FORBIDDEN
FOREST

FORBIDDEN

The Story of Little John and Robin Hood

FOREST

by

Michael Cadnum

ORCHARD · NEW YORK
An imprint of Scholastic Inc.

A NOTE ON SPELLING

The early Robin Hood tales were recorded before English spelling became standardized. The famous outlaw's name itself is spelled variously in early stories: *Robin Whood, Robyn hood, Robyn Hod*. There are many other even more surprising variations. Place names, too, are rendered in many ways. *Kirkslee* is spelled *Kirklees* and *Church Lees*. Sometimes the spelling of a proper name changes in the middle of a given text, like the outlaw himself eluding a reader's eye. My authority for the early tales is R. B. Dobson and J. Taylor's *Rymes of Robyn Hood* (London: Heineman, 1976). Basing my fiction on these venerable ballads, I have chosen the spellings that seem most familiar, or most acceptable, to my eye, remembering all the while that the *grene wode* of legend is a place full of life, forever forbidden, in which literature dwells.

Copyright © 2002 by Michael Cadnum
All rights reserved. Published by Orchard, an imprint of Scholastic Inc.
ORCHARD BOOKS and design are registered trademarks of Orchard Books, Inc.,
a subsidiary of Scholastic Inc. SCHOLASTIC and associated logos are trademarks
and/or registered trademarks of Scholastic Inc.

No part of this publication may be reproduced, or stored in a retrieval
system, or transmitted in any form or by any means, electronic, mechanical,
photocopying, recording, or otherwise, without written permission of the
publisher. For information regarding permission, write to
Orchard, Scholastic Inc., Permissions Department,
555 Broadway, New York, NY 10012.

Library of Congress Cataloging-in-Publication Data
Cadnum, Michael.
Forbidden forest : the story of Little John and Robin Hood : a novel / by Michael
Cadnum.—1st ed. p. cm.
Summary: Profiles Little John, from his quiet life before joining Robin Hood through his
adventures protecting a beautiful lady when she is wrongfully accused of murdering her husband.
ISBN 0-439-31774-6 (alk. paper)
1. Little John (Legendary character)—Juvenile fiction. 2. Robin Hood (Legendary
character)—Juvenile fiction. [1. Little John (Legendary character)—Fiction. 2. Robin Hood
(Legendary character)—Fiction. 3. Great Britain—History—Richard I, 1189–1199—Fiction.
4. Middle Ages—Fiction.] I. Title.
PZ7.C11724   Fo 2002   [Fic]—dc21   2001032932

10 9 8 7 6 5 4 3   02 03 04 05

Printed in the U.S.A.   37
First edition, May 2002
The text of this book is set in 11 point Galliard.

For Sherina

At last
the heron
and its shadow

– Part One –

JOHN LITTLE

Chapter 1

*F*lood spread out over the fields.

Gusts of wind blew cold across plow land silver with water. This was the first sunny day in weeks, and the mud hens swam across the pastures.

A mole tried to make its way across a puddle, flushed from its underground hiding place. Instead of paws, the earth dweller—a soft-furred, eyeless creature—had dark, glovelike appendages, and it struggled, floundering silently in the brown water.

John Little knelt and picked up the struggling animal, no bigger than his thumb. The snouty, helpless creature lifted its head, its heart thrumming wildly in John's palm. In the dark earth, John knew, the animal had a silent, undisturbed kingdom. Here in daylight it was easy prey for fox and cat.

John gently tucked the mole into a mound of turf.

"Hide safely, friend," he said as the mole vanished, tufts of wet soil kicking up in its wake.

A step splashed beside John as he surveyed the wide river. A merchant with two gold rings on his sword hand paused on the sodden bank. "Is it safe to ferry across the river this day?" he asked.

John straightened and looked the merchant up and down. A wool man, by the look of him, garbed in a blue mantle, his kid-leather leggings spotted with mud. John was much taller than the merchant, who drew himself to his full height and looked around for his companions.

"My master and I," said John, "gamble our lives on the river with every crossing."

The current churned. Stones rumbled deep within the river. The angle of a peasant's roof, narrow skeletal timbers, tossed and spun as the river carried it past. A fisher had drowned upriver some three days past, his body stuck in the branches of a drift tree that had carried him by this very bank. John had watched him float by, ravens struggling over his body.

"We'll wait," said the wool man, "for the river to go down."

"It won't go down until Easter," chortled Simon the ferryman, John's master; the holy day was still weeks away. "Come aboard, my lords, all of you."

The travelers hesitated—wisely, John thought. There were four merchants and a sturdily built knight, as well as their horses, placid, stalwart cobs. Months of winter and late winter rains had forced merchants to keep within city walls. Now that spring was here, such men hurried toward London, carrying gold and heavily armed.

Simon chuckled. "We won't let you feel a drop."

The travelers stepped onto the ferry, clinging to their horses and eyeing the tumbling river. At the last moment, as John pushed the ferry away from the bank, another passenger hurried breathlessly onto the vessel.

He was a leathery, quick-moving man with a scar along his neck.

John poled the loaded ferry away from the wharf into the afternoon sunlight. Only a young man of strength could have propelled the vessel forward so steadily. A branch swirled and bobbed in the current. John hefted the pole free of the muddy bottom and plunged it in again, levering the ferry into the middle of the river. This was far more dangerous than any of the well-muscled merchants could guess—one slip, one instant of inattention, and the current would wrestle the ferry downriver.

"Speed, John, right speed or I'll rake a leather strap to your back," said Simon in a cheerful voice.

John gave a nod and sank the ferry pole deep. Simon always threatened dire discipline when passengers were present. But as payment for John's labor, Simon let him sleep in the cottage corner on a rush pallet each night, with broth of eel, river fish, and warm loaves of bread to sup upon, as much as John could want. The ferryman knew rhymes, danced to pipe and song, and could steal the buckle from a burgher's belt while wishing him good day.

John used his strength to propel the ferry forward, closer to the opposite bank, still a far-off gathering of low cottages with thatched roofs, cooking smoke sifting out across the river. It took a strong will and a deft eye to keep the ferry angling toward the staithe, a wharf along the water. The ferry groaned and shrugged as it floated over a half-submerged log, and John set his teeth at the rumble that ran through the vessel.

"John's a hearty lad, but he needs a stout kick to keep him wide awake," said Simon with a laugh, looking at the ferry passengers around him. The merchants chuckled without humor, eager to be free of this lurching ferry.

No other vessel was crossing during this wet, windy season, the rains heavy and the standing water deep, the dairymaids hiking skirts and wading after their herds in the pastures. Only men with a great need to be on the road would be traveling in this early spring wet, and these were men of coin, their sword sheaths chased with silver.

"A right proud gang of rich folk, aren't they?" said Simon in John's ear.

"With purses ready to be lightened," said John in a low voice, accustomed to his master's habits.

"I'll ease that load for them quickly enough," said Simon.

The ferry master coughed richly, pursed his lips, and spat well into the wind so that the morsel of phlegm kissed river current away from any of his passengers. The cautious men huddled together mid-ferry, feet planted solidly, trying to look more confident than they were. John and Simon fell silent at the knight's approach.

John knew what it was like to be far from home, and he could not help feeling a grudging compassion for Simon's patrons. John knew, too, how rough and hard he himself must appear to these soft-handed city men. John was broad shoul-dered and very tall, with a short, sandy-colored young man's beard and close-cropped mud-blond hair. He was called John Little, with the same logic that had his drinking companions call Simon, who was entirely bald, Simon le Hair.

If John still lived in York, folk would know him as John Edwardson, or John Tannerson, or even John Hide, after either his father's Christian name or his trade. His father had been an honest man, dead of a fever three summers past. John had never known his mother, buried in the Fishergate church-yard eighteen winters ago. Now John was a wanderer and a cutpurse, robbing when he was hungry, learning thief-craft from experienced men.

The Crusades in the Holy Land had taken the best knights

and squires for many years now, leaving castle hirelings like these travelers. Some were capable gate men or aging squires, but many were mere house servants hastily trained to wear a sword.

The knight stood close to John as the big youth poled the ferry, and although this man was a head shorter, John could feel the traveler's weight shift the ferry. John pulled the ferry pole from the current and plunged it deep again.

"It takes an iron arm to fight such a flood," said the man-at-arms.

This swordsman had tarried with men of quality, by the sound of it, and had picked up some of the lilting, courteous speech of a castle. John did not like the arrogance and vanity that made men learn gentle accents.

"I could do it easily enough myself," said the man-at-arms agreeably. "But most folk would not be strong enough."

Simon shouldered his way through his passengers, bumped one with a quiet apology, nudged another. Then the ferryman winked at John. The wink was a signal and meant that Simon had already pinched a purse or two, and John clenched his jaw, wishing that Simon had waited until they were closer to the opposite bank before stealing from his passengers.

"You could serve a crusader, ferryman," the knight was saying, making his position in society clear. Only a knight would address another man with this well-intended disdain. "A strong youth like you could surely carry a lance or saddle a horse."

The words gave John a moment of pleasure and pride. Sometimes he had thought that he might have made a good fighting man, given the chance. But John knew that he was destined to be a robber, and little more.

Danger.

He glanced up at the empty blue. Then he hunched forward and peered across the simmering, stone-dark surface of the water. *Unhap,* it was called, an accident woven into the warp of events. You could feel it coming, even when you couldn't guess what it was.

And then he saw it.

A great tree bristled out of the brown river.

It was a huge thing, dark, with the spiky stumps of lopped branches among the growth of new green. It was evidently the work of a sawyer who had hoped to trim and haul this grandfather oak, but lost it to the flood. The surging giant shot out of the muscular river, and John hurried forward, ferry pole ready and gleaming in the afternoon sun.

John tried to tell himself that this was just another bit of drift timber spun along the river by weeks of rain. But he felt his pulse quicken as it coursed closer.

"Saints save us," prayed one of the merchants.

John caught the monster as it leaped from the water, and thrust the ferry pole into the branches, fending the tree away from the vessel. The force of the struggle drove the ferry sideways, and all John's effort could not shove the giant wide. The huge tree rode up, free of the gleaming ferry pole and lifting high, casting a spiked shadow down over the travelers. Even Simon, a veteran of the river, began the first syllables of a prayer.

John swung the massive ferry pole up and held it across his body. The drift tree fell, and he caught it on the staff, but with a sharp and sickening sound the pole broke in two.

The oak giant fell upon John.

Chapter 2

*T*he wool men shrank back, retreating to the far side of the vessel.

Simon stepped forward, one arm out, uttering a further prayer. Only the knight stayed where he was, feet planted wide against the bucking motion of the craft.

John's knees buckled, but he remained standing. His arms embraced the oak, although the girth of the tree was too wide for an encircling hug. John closed his eyes, his cheek pressed flat against the tree. He stood there, silently bearing the weight that pressed all air from his lungs.

John knew that each tree hid within its pith a sprite, a tree soul. He could not guess if this oak still carried its genius within its span, but the young man spoke in his heart, wordlessly, *Help me*. Spare this ferry, and I'll do a deed in return.

John wrestled the log along the length of the ferry, straining, grunting. The effort made his sinews burn and dimmed his vision.

He cast the tree into the boiling current.

"Heaven be praised!" said one of the travelers, his voice shaking.

John fell to his knees. His rough-spun tunic was wet, and scales of bark clung to his sleeves. His breath came in ragged gasps.

And now the promised gesture was required.

He took Simon's hand as he climbed to his feet, and pulled the ferryman to the ferry's rail. "Give them back their silver," whispered John.

"What are you saying?" hissed Simon. Then, for the benefit of the merchants and the knight, he added, "I'll buy a pitcher of the finest spring ale for you tonight, John, for your brave effort. And a pot of mead."

A spare pole, a flimsy length of wood, was strapped to the rail, and John could not speak for a moment, in a hurry to free the pole and dig it hard into the river bottom, driving the ferry ever closer to its destination.

John levered the ferry hard, and said, keeping his voice low, "Give them back what you have taken."

A figure stiffened nearby, the knight just close enough to catch John's words.

"Quiet, John," Simon hissed.

Then he made a show of laughing, like a man at ease. But the knight turned and murmured something to his fellow travelers. The merchants began a hurried inventory of their purses and cloak fastenings, and more than one of them gave a bitter exclamation.

The knight lifted a hand and let it fall on Simon's shoulder, seized him, and lifted him, one foot dangling like a market-day puppet.

Just then the ferry lurched, and the wharf assistant, a quiet man habitually half paralyzed with ale, tossed a loosely knotted rope in John's general direction.

The young man caught the rope and hauled the vessel close to the wharf. The ferry bumped the pilings hard, but the knight had thrown Simon onto the deck and planted a knee on the ferryman's chest while he searched the pockets and hiding places of Simon's loose-fitting tunic.

The knight's searching fingers brought out a dull silver pin and a sack fat with gold marks, the gold making its distinctive chuckle within the leather as the man-at-arms tossed it in his hand.

Simon protested that these treasures were his own, but two outraged merchants identified their possessions, and the knight reached into his cloak and brought forth a long, slender blade—a finishing knife, the customary weapon for cutting the throats of the half-slain.

John could not see far enough into the future to know if the knight was going to cut Simon's throat. Surely the blade pressed Simon's flesh, and the indented skin reddened, blood starting.

John seized the knight by his bright hair and yanked his head back, hard.

The man-at-arms rose halfway to his feet, his eyes round, hands reaching out into the air. The blade fell clattering to the deck as the rig-bone within the knight's neck gave a snap. At the ugly sound, John released his hold on the man. The knight dropped to the deck, his eyes wide. The knight's feet jerked and spasmed, and a pool of piss spread out around the body.

John straightened. All his life he had heard firelight tales, heroes slaying ogres and errant knights. He had never committed such an act himself. John uttered a prayerful "Blessed Mary!" and gazed down at his own two hands. John's horror kept him standing where he was, unable to make a further sound.

Simon knelt beside the knight, feeling the body for pulse,

for breath. The ferryman said, hoarsely, "He'll be well—have no cares, good wool men. Disembark, and God speed you."

John could not swim, and he dreaded the thought of his body sinking down into the current. But he heard the low, promising voice of the river: *Come away, come away.*

The ferryman looked up at John and said, for the benefit of the travelers, "The good knight needs room, please; stand back."

John could hear the voice in Simon's soul, the urgent message, *Run!*

The merchants had John in their arms before the young man could move. John accepted the justice of this. He had taken the life of a man of quality, and the blows fell on John's shoulders and arms—fists and then sword butts, and then the flats of the swords as the merchants freshened to their task.

The sweating wool men shoved John up the riverbank, laboring at him with their swords, nicking a shoulder, drawing blood from a knee. Each bite of steel cut a little deeper into flesh. John stumbled over tree roots, treading through puddles.

The riverside hamlet was called Stoneford, a place where men and pigs lived in neighborly contentment. Now the village stirred, men and women interrupted in their afternoon labors by the curses of the merchants. A woman with a wort paddle, in the midst of brewing beer, gaped at the sight of a young man accepting punishment without complaint.

Suffering was best endured in silence. John knew this, as did every well-churched soul under the sky. Heaven sent us pain to let us experience what Our Lord knew, a spike through each blessed hand. Illness and injury: each buffet sent by Heaven was a gift. Especially in a case like this, when John knew that the punishment was entirely fair. A man-killer deserved the harshest justice.

And yet John was growing angry.

"Easy, good sirs," said a nearby wife, portly in her apron. "Whatever the crime this giant lad has committed, let us fetch the sheriff's men."

"No need," said the stoutest of merchants, drawing back his blade. John wrapped his hand around the sword-wielding arm and gripped hard. The merchant grinned with effort, but his hand released the blade. John picked up the weapon, the hilt warm and moist with grip sweat. John was not accustomed to hefting a sword, but the weight of the weapon was pleasing.

He broke free and began to run, splashing through pig soil, hens squawking, geese fleeing. Grass whipped his leggings, and a village dog, a yellow creature with a tight-curled tail, ran along with John, barking. John left the dog far behind.

He stumbled, and caught himself from falling into the shadowy shaft of a water-well hidden in the grass. Many villages had such old wells, a constant source of accident. A stone dislodged by his step ticked the echoing interior, and long moments after John left it behind he could hear the splash.

The cries of the merchants and their hurrying footsteps began to fade as John hurried into the thick saplings along the verge of the woods. He ran until the sounds of pursuit dimmed.

The forest, came the elf cries around him.

Into the forest, run.

As John approached the woods, some peace-loving human part of him hesitated.

Every honest man knew that the greenwood was the haunt of desperate men who were outlawed, declared beyond the protection of the law. The forest was also the refuge of the wood sprites, centuries old, who lived in the ground far from the eyes of men.

John looked back. The merchants were pointing, indicating across the sodden meadow a track that anyone could see, the thick grass parted all the way to where John panted, sword in hand.

Every woodland in the kingdom was forbidden to folk of common birth, and much of the forest was royal hunting land. To set foot in such a wood was to break the law.

John turned and, lifting the branch of a young elm, entered the green dark.

Chapter 3

John ran hard, leaves tearing at his face, twigs slashing. Sheriff's men on a manhunt often used wolfhounds bred to nose a criminal in a hayrick or a copse of beeches. John reckoned that he would be able to survive one night, or two, before the hounds found him and tore him to pieces.

John drank from a stream that tasted of soil and green leaves, and followed the brook, simmering and powerful as all running water in the land this stormy season. John hoped the fast-running water would make it more difficult for the dogs to follow his scent.

When the shadowy wood grew darker still and the air cold, he climbed into a tree. His gashes and bruises ached, and a runnel of blood tickled him as it seeped from a wound in his knee. He stayed there in the crotch of the spreading branches, the hint of silver daylight far to the west fading, vanishing.

This was not the first time he was homesick for the walls of York. With his father dead, and his family's servant Hilda mocked and more than once pilloried for trading in graveyard bones and other magic relics, John had grown restless for the world beyond the town. Now he would have accepted the lowliest station of stable lad in any town to get out of these wet woods alive.

The weight of the sword in his belt was cold and foreign, and John felt the hard oak bark dig into his tunic and his rough wool leggings. He hated the unfamiliar whisper of the wind in the trees. Or was it the wind? Like any Christian, John knew that the devil was at home in any wild place, and here John could expect no watchman's vigil or ale brewer's fellowship.

John slept, and as he slept he had a dream.

The tree he embraced transformed, in this dream, into a woman. This beautiful tree dame held John, and he coupled with her the way husband mates with wife.

Some holy men were said to have divine visions, saints with fiery swords. Hilda, rolling out the crust for squab pie, had said that a dream of a skylark's song, high above, foretold wealth. John had known an innkeeper's daughter, one rainy night, and a hayward's widow, once, under the blue sky. Perhaps there was a woman waiting somewhere for him, a kind, beautiful forester's daughter.

John woke sweating, clinging to the branch of the tree. His cuts throbbed. The dark was perfect. He climbed upward, even higher into the tree, and clung, wide awake until dawn.

Birdsong celebrated sunlight, high above—especially the jaunty, throaty notes of the woodcock, and the brazen cackle of rooks. John's father had loved birds, often stopping his work, loading a cart with stiff hides, to listen to a distant cuckoo. John had made his father laugh by imitating the blackbird's song. But now even this bird chatter made John cautious. Hilda used to slice parsnips in the kitchen and tell John that elves put on the voices of crows and such creatures when they wanted to caution humans, or to laugh at them.

John inched downward, stiff, the fresh scabs on his cuts worried by the rough bark of the oak. But something prompted him to breathe thanks to the tree, and to whatever spirits of the wood might be nearby.

He was nearly all the way to the ground when a sound stilled him, and he crouched in an elbow of the oak.

For a long moment he heard only birds, and the great silence of daylight lifting the night mist upward, through the green canopy above. But then John heard it again, the jeering alarm—rooks taking flight, complaining.

A whispered step.

A silent wake through the chitter of birds.

Two figures slipped into view. One was dressed in the worn brown leggings and leather cap of a country yeoman, a man of property who had to sweat for his daily bread. But this sun-bronzed man was following a trail, and it did not take John more than a heartbeat to recognize the weathered stranger with the scarred neck, the last passenger to join the ferry the day before.

The yeoman had a companion now, a man in a gray traveler's cloak and hood, red silk gleaming at the sleeves. The silent figure walked well behind the careful yeoman.

John found his hand on the hilt of his newly possessed weapon. The yeoman had a staff, and wore a sword in his belt. John crept down from his tree, and he realized, with deep unease, how chilled and sweaty his hands were, and how rapidly his breath came and went.

He stepped away from the protective oak and took a stand in a clearing. The yeoman straightened from a crouch on the root-scored earth, and put out a hand to catch the cloaked man's eye.

"Good morning, outlaw," said the man of quality. His red silk sleeves were brilliant in the forks of sunlight that fell from above.

Each man had an apportioned place in life, and this place was more essential to a man's value upon earth than his Christian name. It was polite to address a stranger by his calling—chandler, silversmith—but it was strange to hear *outlaw* used in this formal way.

John gave a short bow, as was polite and wise when meeting a man of worth, but he offered no spoken courtesy. Although he had long envied men of guile and cunning, John knew his own skills were more straightforward. He had a strong back and a hard fist. Smart men stole the world away, while men like John could only dream.

"I am the lord of Kirkslee," said the gray-cloaked traveler. He had a soft voice and the pale, lined face of a seneschal or Exchequer's man, someone accustomed to taxes and expenditures. "I am called Red Roger. This is my man, Tom Dee."

Tom Dee made a leg, thrusting one foot forward and bowing, a show of castle manners. He was sun-browned, with cheerful features, but his eyes measured John and he took a half step back, setting his staff across his body. Despite his show of caution, John liked him at once.

There were famous outlaws of the forest. Red Roger, a legendary nobleman-robber, was one. Another was a shadowy, much-rumored figure, a man who reputedly mocked his victims more energetically than he robbed them. This mysterious robber of legend was known as Robin Wood, or Hood. John did not believe such a man really lived at all, outside the world of ballads.

But he would not have imagined Red Roger was a real man, either. "Good morning to you," said John, resting his hand on his sword hilt. He did not add "my lord," although he did offer his own name.

"The sheriff's men will be hunting you, John Little," said Roger, reaching within his cloak to withdraw a wedge of bread loaf. "You are famous in taverns and inns overnight: John Little, the Killer Giant."

"As Heaven's Queen wills it," said John, a phrase that came to him without effort, one of his father's heartfelt half-prayers when a shipment of green hides arrived rotten, or well chewed by rats.

"They hunt with dogs," said Tom Dee. He was not much younger than his master, but looked weather-hardened, the old scar along the side of his neck the result of a knife that had just missed what every butcher knew was the life vein.

John seized the bread from the nobleman's hand and ate eagerly. The loaf was made of beans and bran, not the fine white flour John had expected.

"Come with us and we will save you from a noose of new rope," said Red Roger. He had the easy, straightforward gaze of a man too jaded to be any danger in combat. Although not frail, he had a priest's manner of half smiling before he spoke, as though to make the inevitable fall gently.

"Indeed," said John, "my father raised a son who stands straight." This was a marketplace phrase for an able-bodied worker, and John realized as he uttered it how out of place such a remark sounded in this wild wood.

Tom Dee laughed. "They'll loose the wolfhounds on your hams and you'll stand like a snake." *Stonde lyk an snaca.*

John gave the two of them what he hoped was a manly smile. He would be grateful to become a part of such a legendary outlaw's band, but John sensed that a man so famous for breaking the law could not be trusted.

Red Roger raised a hand and listened.

"We are too late," said Tom Dee with a sharp little laugh, like a man about to enjoy a cockfight.

John was thankful that dogs were not falcons. With a hunting fowl, death falls silently, a gauntlet from Heaven. These hunting dogs approached fast, giving tongue to their discovery of John's scent, and while it gripped him to his heart to know they brought death, he prepared his soul with a prayer, his sword in his hand.

The first dog to burst through the trees was a shaggy, long-bodied beast, a smaller hunting dog at his flank. Tom Dee strode into the dogs with his short sword, and the two dogs soon kicked, shivering. One by one the others broke stride, biting at the air, scratching with a hind foot, or reaching back with a peeled muzzle to pluck at a gash in the flank as Tom slipped among them. Even the ones that reared, growling, soon coughed red as Tom lunged and slashed, making quick work.

Only one dog, a deerhound, managed to avoid Tom's blade, and as this beast approached, Lord Roger drew a sword from under his cloak. Like a trick the nobleman and the dog had practiced for months, the sword blade plunged all the way into the animal's ribs.

The deerhound's jaws snapped, the animal lunging and kicking. Red Roger did nothing to ease the hound's agony, and it was Tom who stepped in and finished the dying animal, a quick stroke with his blade.

The deerhound bled from a cut that exactly matched the scar in Tom's throat, and John had the uneasy sense that Tom Dee was a dead man given life by some unknown power.

But the look Tom Dee gave him was that of a living man, and a friendly one at that. "Hurry, John Little, or their swords will make you smaller yet."

Chapter 4

The three men slipped from root to root across the forest floor. Then they doubled back, so close to the hunters that the voices of men still lively from breakfast wine reached them through the trees. The searchers were angry, beating the brush, calling in coarse language.

The three approached the hamlet of Stoneford, but kept to the shade of the young elms. A cache of equipment rested in a grove of saplings, and Red Roger sorted through old, well-worn armor. He placed a brass and leather helmet on John's head, and fastened a ragged skirt of mail around the youth's middle. Then he murmured a word into Tom Dee's ear, and the yeoman slipped through the meadow grass and was gone.

Sometimes the sound of hunters' voices reached them, and Red Roger lifted a finger to his lips. Sometimes the leather armor of a sheriff's man gleamed darkly at the edge of the wood, the man eyeing the too badly trampled earth or letting his horse crop meadow grass. Then Red Roger would go down on one knee and grow very still, and John likewise would crouch in the grass and wait for their solitude to grow perfect again.

Tom Dee returned with three horses: a bay cob, a gelding with one blind eye, and a dray horse big enough to be a knight's mount but heavy-hoofed and sullen. The gelding lifted his head and pranced at Red Roger's touch, and the bay cob settled well enough under the yeoman.

But John, who had ridden only one horse in his life, and that only after he had drunk a bellyful of strong ale, put his foot into a stirrup and froze. The horse sneezed, the convulsion running through the bulk of the big animal. Realizing that their pursuers could approach at any moment, John swung up into the saddle with a pounding heart.

Tom Dee laughed. "A man-at-arms holds his elbows so," he said, demonstrating a poised, steady posture, arms crooked. "And he keeps his feet in his stirrups, except to kick a peasant's head."

The dray swelled and let out a huge sigh. John's chain mail chimed at each clop of the big horse's hooves. His feet dangled far below the stirrups, and he feared the mount might give out under his weight. "How much did you pay for this worthy dray?" asked John, not wishing to offend.

"The horse displeases you?" asked Tom.

"I pray you have not been cheated," John replied in the manner of the best merchant foister, a hard bargainer.

"The price was sweet," said Tom. "They cost our Lord Roger not a farthing."

"Tell me, Tom," said John, afraid to put the question into words, "what happened to Simon the ferryman?"

"Your master had few friends," said Tom Dee.

"What do you suppose happens when merchants get their hands on a thief?" asked Red Roger. "They cut him to chops, and let him bleed to death without a priest."

John clenched his fists, a gesture so sudden his horse gave a kick.

A sheriff's man rode up the High Way on a cob horse curried and clipped, a pretty thing. Lord Roger glanced back and made a soft click with his tongue, like a man chiding a dog. Tom Dee gave a tight smile and said, "John, say not a word, and take this goatskin in your hand. Make believe you've had more than a swallow of sweet wine."

John accepted the skin of wine from Tom's hand.

The deputy took in John's poor knightly disguise with one glance. The lawman's horse, with its soft mouth and quick hooves, stretched its muzzle toward John's dray, and the sheriff's man twitched his reins. Lord Roger swept back his cloak, letting his silver buckles and brilliant red sleeves take the sun.

This flash of aristocratic manner momentarily silenced the sheriff's man, and when he questioned them at last, Red Roger was brief in his reply.

"Yes, we heard of this outlaw youth," said Red Roger in a nobleman's drawl. "We tried to find a pitcher of wine worth drinking at Stoneford, and the place was a hive of rumor— no place for a quiet drinker today."

The lawman's eyes were full of questions, but Red Roger gave his horse a pat and explained that the High Way from York was a ragtag mess of robbers and beggars, "no honest man in sight."

"My lord," began the sheriff's man, staring hard at John. Then the deputy broke into a grin. "I do believe your young sergeant is drunk."

"Drunk as a boar, and I'm out of patience," said Roger. "I'm packing him off to Jerusalem, where the pagans can stew him in oil."

It was not true just then, but it became the truth as John mourned his thieving master the ferryman, a man with a warm laugh. John emptied the goatskin, drinking hard.

The morning became a blur of sunlight and bright puddles as the wine fumes gripped him. He was certain that he fell off the horse sometime in the forenoon, but he had no sure memory of it.

At some hour during the afternoon John lay flat in an open wagon, the wooden wheels creaking, rimmed with highway mud. The wagon carried the sweet smell of timber, and splinters lay about the wagon bed.

Red Roger held up John's head and let him drink from a skin of wine and water. He said, "Rest easy, John."

Red Roger looked up sharply and said, "Swing wide of the ruts, will you?"

The driver's voice responded, in singsong obedience, "Yes, my lord."

"You'll stay with me, John," said Red Roger. "I'll teach you to rob from the very angels."

Chapter 5

*N*o cartwheels turned, no axle rumbled. The world was still.

John was in a bedchamber. Red Roger held a cup, and John swallowed a thin, sweet liquor. "Pears steeped with Damascus prunes," he said. "Sound medicine for a confused mind."

"Prayers," John heard himself say. The proper prayers were as necessary as medicine for recovery, he knew. Saint James was the saint to aid the ill, and John remembered praying with Hilda as his father lay gasping in his bed. "Must pray," said John.

Or perhaps he thought it so urgently it was like a spoken word. Surely no Christian had ever experienced such a headache.

John opened his eyes. A wax candle burned, giving brilliant light. The bedchamber had stone walls. John could smell the rain outside as it touched the mortar and rock and pattered on the shuttered window.

He stood and put a hand out to a woven cloth on the wall

to keep from falling. His sword cuts still ached, but with the itchy soreness that promises healing. The bright colors of the dyed wool at his hand depicted a glorious battle, a castle, and a man lifting a trumpet to his lips. Beyond, hills were spiked with armed men. This was, John reckoned, the Battle of Jericho. The walls of the besieged city were about to tumble, and the army of the Lord about to hack its enemy to scallops.

John was hungry. A young woman garbed in rough-spun beige wool entered the room with the cautionary step of an experienced house servant. She was dimpled and pink-cheeked. "Oh, you're awake, are you?"

John admitted that he was awake, and standing.

"I'll tell his lordship," said the serving woman.

When the door whispered on its hinges again, Red Roger entered the room.

"I cannot repay you with more than thanks, my lord," John began. Polite formula, but entirely true.

"I know you'll repay me very well, John," said Lord Roger with a quiet laugh.

John sat in a large room. His father had done business with respectable pelterers and river merchants, and as a boy John had entered well-timbered houses. But this was in size a grander dwelling than any he had dined in before, and the roast hare and onions was the best dish he had tasted since his father sealed a contract with the archbishop's armorer.

Lord Roger did not take a bite of hare, but he joined John in drinking wine, and answered John's questioning glances with a calm "No one followed us here."

John drank as much of the white wine as he could hold. It was served by a manservant with lowered gaze and barely whispered apologies as he removed John's plate and checked the contents of the pitcher. The serving woman tiptoed in, her eyebrows raised in apology, and lit an oil lamp with a glowing twist of dried rushes.

There were no other servants, judging from the silence of the rooms in the big house. And aside from the lord there were no other inhabitants, no children or lady of the house. The walls were cloaked with noble hangings, woven illustrations of unicorns and miracles. But there were few furnishings, aside from the table and two benches. The dishes and candle fittings were of finest quality, but one platter was old silver, roughly smithed, and a candleholder on the table was decorated with the faces of angels. Not one piece of silver matched another.

"Moses is striking water from a rock," said Lord Roger. John stood, aware now that his gaze had seemed to be on the decorated cloth at one end of the room. "The Children of Israel are parched, in a desert. Do you know the story?"

"Well enough, my lord." Once, long ago, Father Chad had given the lesson in simple Latin, and John had followed the meaning.

Perhaps this answer did not please his lordship, for his eyes were suddenly downcast.

"But," said John quickly, "I forget much."

"Life under Heaven is a wilderness," said Red Roger. "We have no true companions, John. You will need new garments. Undyed gray and Lincoln green. Find Tom and take him with you to cut a quarterstaff. And tell him you'll need a skinner's knife or short sword—something with a fine edge."

John realized that he had not seen his sword on awakening, and put his hand to his hip.

"A staff and knife, John, are the tools you need," said Lord Roger. "Your work will be silent. We aren't men of wild song and the longbow, like those beggarly thieves of Sherwood Forest."

"Are there such outlaws?" asked John.

Red Roger gazed into the fire. "Only," he said at last, "until men like you and I can run them down."

Chapter 6

*O*utside the presence of Red Roger, Tom Dee was an even quicker, more agreeable man. He was eager to show John his lordship's land, the henhouses bare of a single fowl, the pond with only a few ducks, all the way to a peasant's cottage, its roof bare of thatch, the beams naked.

"He has only the two servants," said Tom, "Albert and Freda, Albert's daughter. A rare cutpurse was Albert, in all the big towns. The sheriff of Doncaster's men beat him and left him in a ditch for dead."

"It is kind of Red Roger," said John, "to shelter a fugitive."

Tom gave a short laugh. "As for Freda, she can make a noise like a woodcock, exactly."

"Why are there no other servants?" asked John.

"A bright pearl like Freda," said Tom, with a smile, "who can make a noise like a wild pigeon, is worth three giant men like you. Red Roger finds the men he needs, and no more."

Tom led the way back to his own cottage, a white-walled, low building with a smoke vent in the roof. It was dark inside, and John could barely make out Tom as he searched among what sounded like tools of iron and wood. Hand pikes, halberds, and several glaives—soldiers' spears. "This quarterstaff I took from a yeoman from the west, a man not quite as tall as you but wide. See how it fits your grip."

John stepped into the sunlight with the staff. Whoever had once owned it, he had not used it much—the wood was smooth, both ends unworn. John swung it at an imaginary foe. A staff like this could dent a crusader's helmet.

"And this knife will suit you," said Tom. It was a horn-handled blade, whetted keen, and big enough to skin a fallow deer.

Now Tom's voice grew quiet, confiding. "We must be careful. The law cannot hurt a man like his lordship," he said. "He can act the nobleman, bored and above lifting a purse. But it can lay its hands on me, and on you. I saw a man gutted with a pickax in Derby for using it to dig under a baron's wall."

Executioners often used a felon's tools against him during punishment, and John had seen equally dramatic examples in York, in the fields outside Micklegate Bar.

"When we go out," Tom continued, "stay right with me, step by step. Keep to the shadows. If ever you hear me call out for you to flee, then flee hard, John, and never once look back." *Fli herd, John.*

"Surely his lordship's enemies are mine," said John. He said this with enthusiasm—loyalty was considered a great virtue. "But I will not take a man's life," he added.

"Red Roger is a proud man, and unforgiving," said Tom. "He'll never forget a slight, as long as he breathes. I warn you: never insult or hurt him. He lives for the pleasure of punishing his enemies."

"Then I hope I am always his friend," said John with an uneasy chuckle.

"You are a dog to Red Roger," said Tom, "and so am I—strong and loyal. His lordship has no friends."

"The abbot of Saint Phocas is ill famed," said Tom Dee, "with a woman he keeps in his parish house. And he has a whore here in Barnsdale, an innkeeper's dimpled daughter. He rides to see her each Monday—he's a steady sinner."

They sat in Tom's cottage, John's eyes growing accustomed to the dark interior and the eye-smarting wood smoke. They ate oatcakes and mare's-milk cheese.

"The priest is sunk deep in harlotry," Tom continued, not unhappily. "And he cheats at dice. Raffle and three-dice, any game, and cards too. Our abbot would play toss-coin at the gates of Heaven. He is a smarter gambler than Red Roger, and the lordship hates him."

"He carries coin at his belt," said John, understanding what he was being told.

"But the abbot rides a-whoring with an armed guard," said Tom. "Red Roger has been hoping for a strong-armed robber like you."

Freda stood in the courtyard, head to one side, and when a woodcock began its song, she echoed it, note for note. *You'll weep, lady, no more*—this was what some people heard in the bird's soft tune.

She knocked a turnip on its head, three times for each meager pink-and-ivory root, the only vegetable in this early spring.

John could close his eyes and see the gardens of his boyhood. Leeks and just-cropped colewort, parsley and a row of garlic. Hilda gathering tansy to use against fleas, the flowers dried and tied in a cloth sack.

An unchurched household, Lord Roger's house observed neither meatless days nor Sunday worship, and this sabbath morning John worked beside Freda, clearing the garden of weeds. A worm spilled out of a clod, onto a stepping stone, and Freda rescued the squirming blind creature from the sun, where it would surely parch and die. She flung it onto the moist, dark garden clods, and then bent to her work again.

When John spied a crack in the garden wall, he remembered what Hilda had called such fissures. "Look, an elf gate," he said lightly.

Freda straightened and looked him straight in the face.

"They come in from the hill," she said at last. "At night."

John felt a prickle, and a chill.

"To watch us?" he asked at last.

Freda smiled. She laughed and bent back to her work.

John was sure she had forgotten, but much later, as they raked the pulled weeds into a mound, she said, "There's not a thing we do that the elves would want to look at. But even so—they know everything."

Was it a trick of his mind, or was she telling him something more?

Sang the woodcock, *You're in danger, John, yes you are.*

Chapter 7

"Like children, but not." That was how Hilda had described elves she had seen as a little girl, in the field near the hamlet of Bodeton Percy.

Hilda had caught a fever after sitting in the pillory outside Bootham Bar in York, and she died shriven and forgiven by the priest for her trade in hanged men's knuckles. But the treatment of an *elf frecht*—an elf friend—was hard in most cities, and John had been happy to take to the road after Hilda's death. John, too, would have faced punishment someday. Only hunger had forced him to leap onto a passing cheese man's cart one warm noon, carve a slice from a great golden wheel, and run off into the hedges. That was his first, negligible act of thievery. And it was far from his last.

Day by day John had found that the drunken chamberlain and the road-weary traveling clerk did not notice the slits in their purses until long afterward, much less remember the tall youth jostling them in the market.

John rarely let himself imagine finding a red-cheeked wife,

bedding down with her on long wintry nights, and living cozily in a cottage. But John suffocated every such hope in his breast. He knew that a criminal's life ended with a trudge up a ladder, a bowed head, and a hangman's yellow-rope noose.

The following afternoon, after an early supper of pottage and brown bread, and a pitcher of thick brown ale, John followed Tom into the shadows. He felt a tug at his sleeve, and turned to see Freda.

She waited until Tom was well out of earshot. Then she pressed an amulet into John's hand.

The amulet was a heavy base metal crudely smithed in the shape of a cross. John shook it and something sealed inside its hollow core made a rattling whisper.

"The finger of a man who killed his master," she said. "Hanged and quartered, all without a murmur." A good death was much admired, and the relics of a penitent criminal were considered powerful magic.

"Good Freda, I doubt that I need such great protection."

Smelling of yeast and sweat, she put her lips to his ear, and kissed it, just as Hilda used to.

"What did our sweet Freda give you?" asked Tom Dee.

John showed him the amulet, then returned it to safekeeping around his neck.

"Do you admire our lord and master?" asked Tom.

"He must be cunning," said John, after giving the question some thought.

A stone wall ran across the hill, and a flock of sheep, each beast with its head to the turf, grazed in the distant mist. Some stewards had burned out villages for the grazing land,

and John could see the dark stumps of cottage walls. Wool was a more profitable crop than barley or peas, and only a few shepherds were required to work a flock.

"He unsnared me from a mantrap a year ago last Candlemas," said Tom Dee. "I tried to live by poaching venison, and now I serve him as he desires."

"You must feel grateful to him," said John.

Tom did not respond for a while, the two men approaching a disused wellhead, the watering place timbered over, a flat, grassless place in the field.

At last he said, "Our Lord Roger has no warmth like other men."

"But he is kind to you," said John, feeling embarrassed as he spoke for his own lack of worldliness.

"And he beds Freda," said Tom, "but this is not the same as love."

"Whose land is this?" asked John, eyeing a cottage space reduced to char and ash. He was troubled by this insight into the passions of Lord Roger, and for the moment he did not want to hear any more.

"Our own Lord Red Roger's," said Tom. "He drove his peasants off the land, and does well at sheep breeding. But he plays at dice."

"So he is always hungry for coin," said John.

"Always. And if we don't hurry," said Tom, "the abbot will outrun us."

Chapter 8

They waited in the long shadows.

A black bird, too solitary to be a rook but too quiet to be a crow, settled on a rut in the road before them and eyed the two men. John cast pebbles at the bird, but the winged creature took a few steps to one side, bounded across a rut ridge, and parted its beak in silence.

"They'll know we're here," said John.

Tom Dee had to laugh. "The bird is going to warn them?"

"Birds are great traitors to a hunter," said John. "As a seasoned poacher you should know that much. You go out with your snare or your fowling bow, and a crow is tattling to the hare and to the grouse."

"It's a bird," said Tom in friendly exasperation. "They don't wake up every morning with the need to worry us. Besides, I never told you I was skilled at poaching, only that I tried my hand at it."

John crouched beside a large and healthy gray nettle

bush, the largest he had ever seen. He folded his arms around his knees to avoid its touch.

The land here was sparsely forested, and shrubs and low plants, dock and spreading hawthorn bushes, were the only cover. When the sound of hooves reached them, it might have been a flaw in the wind—no horses appeared.

The High Way stretched north, watery ruts gleaming in the muted sunset. John crouched with Tom as he held one end of a rope running across the road, the other end knotted around a fence post. Again, the sound of trotting horses, but the road remained empty. The bird departed at last, circling high and vanishing.

When the riders appeared it was without warning, the horses nearly upon Tom and John.

The abbot and his armed companion rode hard through the sudden light rain. The clergyman must have guessed, or perhaps his companion. Or perhaps John gave them away, standing upright to pull on the rope. One of the men made a sound, an intake of breath.

John heaved hard on the rope, stretching the heavy cord across the road. The abbot was a good horseman and did not saw at the reins. His horse careened, turning to one side. John set his feet, and it took all his strength to bear the weight of the steed as it stumbled and fell, spilling its rider to the ground just as the hemp rope broke.

The abbot's armed companion struck at Tom with a spear, but missed. Tom seized the fighting man's leg and dragged him from this horse. The man lashed at the yeoman with the length of his spear, and rammed the butt into Tom's midsection, but the yeoman tripped him without much effort and sat on his chest as the man bawled for the abbot to ride hard.

The abbot's tough but worn out with lechery, Tom had promised. *It will be easy work.*

John straddled the churchman. He reached into the sweating abbot's tunic, found nothing, groped his cloak for hidden silver, felt nothing again, and finally worked at removing a carnelian-and-gold ring from the man's hand.

The flushed, fuming abbot glared as he lay flat on the ground, breathing hard. "So the robber hires giants, now, to cut throats," he said.

"Your blood will stay in your body," said John, grunting, as he tried to pry the ring over the knob of the abbot's knuckle. The abbot wore only a signet ring, used to seal documents and score contracts, and the pretty carnelian ring on his little finger.

Tom had pried the helmet off the gray-haired guard and was beating the armed man about the face with the butt of his knife.

"Here!" said the abbot, snatching the ring from his little finger and throwing it at John.

John caught it, and examined the blood-bright stone and the delicate work of the setting. It was a lady's ring. Tom was still hammering the guardsman's thick gray hair, and blood was flowing.

"That man's head is too thick," called John. "Leave him."

Tom looked hard at his companion, argument in his eyes.

John slipped the ring into his pocket. Tom rose to his feet, breathing hard. "I'll need to have a word with our good abbot, John. You may wait down the road."

The knife in Tom's hand was blue and bright, fresh-whetted that morning.

"You will not spill his blood," cautioned John, climbing to his feet and standing protectively over the abbot.

"Why would I so much as prick him?" said Tom. "I only want to give him a message from Lord Roger." Tom smiled apologetically.

Tom was going to kill the abbot, John knew. Why else would he be so careless, uttering his lordship's name?

Tom shrugged. "Walk on down the road, John," he said, almost kindly. "I'll join you soon."

John's staff was on the muddy road two strides away. His knife was in its scabbard at his side, but a cross-belly reach to tug it free from the new leather scabbard would take a long moment.

The abbot said, "Heaven honors mercy." His voice was gentle even now, although breathy and thin.

"Listen to the fat lecher begging for his life," said Tom cheerfully. "Have you ever heard such a cowardly sinner?" He gave the churchman a kick, and the abbot's breath was ragged. The man rolled to one side, unable to utter the words that twisted his lips.

John seized Tom's tunic, gathered it in his fist, and half raised the yeoman to his toes. *Do not touch him again.*

John never said the words.

He saw it happen, as clearly as a story-play on market day, a pantomime acted out in deliberate step by step. The guard rose up on one knee, wincing with the effort. He gripped his spear and steadied the weapon. Such heavy spears were never thrown, to John's knowledge, but always used from horseback.

Before John could move, or speak a word, the iron-tipped spear was in the air.

Chapter 9

John carried Tom Dee across the hill in the growing darkness, the injured man's breath rattling in and out of his body. Blood streamed from the spear wound in Tom's back, soaking into John's tunic, and several times Tom tried to speak.

"We're almost home," John said.

John knew his prayers well enough, and said them, and he trusted that with speed and the grace of Heaven there was still hope. But when he paused to give Tom water from a stream, the wounded man's lips were cold, and his legs and hands were icy. Everyone knew that death began with the toes and the fingers and marched inward, toward the lungs.

Tom gave a half smile, a hitch of one corner of his mouth, and spoke. The words were unmistakable, but John said, with a forced laugh, "We'll have plenty of time to talk over ale, Tom, around the fire."

"Fly, John," Tom said without sound.

Flee Lord Roger.

The wounded man was a heavy load, and sometimes he gripped John's sleeve in pain or as he tried to communicate some urgent further word. Tom seized the amulet around John's neck, and held it the way an infant holds a paternal finger, or a sick man his crucifix.

Help me, Heaven, prayed John silently.

And to the grass and hawthorn, the stones and tree stumps, he added in a low voice, as Hilda had taught him, "Help me, creatures of the hill." But Tom's limbs went slack, and his mouth gaped, opening and closing with every stride, although he still breathed.

John burst into the great house and stretched Tom, still bleeding, on the rush-strewn floor. "You can't lay him here," spat Albert. "Blood from here to the road, and every sheriff's dog on your trail."

"No one followed," said John.

Albert was not servile, and he did not smile. His voice was hard. "Get that bleeding man out of here."

John carried Tom to the injured man's cottage. Lord Roger arrived just after Tom stopped breathing. John let his friend's body lie flat, now that the wound would cause no pain. He folded the yeoman's hands over his breast, the broad hands and square fingers gentle now, and still. He pressed the amulet into the peaceful hands of his friend, the cross with the single knucklebone. Tom had died unshriven, unable to breathe his sins into the ear of a priest.

His lordship's leather leggings were wet from riding, and he carried red kid gloves in one hand. "Have you ever run down a stoat, John?" he asked.

John was in deep sorrow, and he expected the nobleman to share his grief.

"Of course you have not," said his lordship, answering

his own question. "Devilish creature, smart as a ferret, and stronger."

John waited while the nobleman raised the blanket and gazed down at Tom's peaceful, pale features, so unlike the ruddy, alert expression he had worn in life.

"Is the abbot still alive?" asked Lord Roger after a long silence.

"When I left him he was sitting in the mud," said John. *Putting the carnelian ring back on his finger,* he did not add.

"Did Tom not understand my instructions?"

"Tom Dee," said John, "was not the only man on the High Way this evening."

Lord Roger let the blanket fall and did not speak at once.

"I'm thirsty," he said at last.

John stayed where he was, settling the rough wool blanket over the face of Tom Dee.

"Have some pigeon pie and a pitcher of wine with me," said Lord Roger. "I'll find better men than Tom, and richer quarry than the abbot."

John had heard that many lords had less feeling than peasants, and that some men of quality never wept. He had not believed it, until now.

"My lord, I'm leaving your service," said John. The speech was simple, but it had a deliberate legal character, the formal parting of a serving man with his master. He rose to his feet.

"You can't, John."

A man could be bound to his lord for a period of service, perhaps an entire lifetime. "You found me free, my lord, and I joined you willingly," said John.

Lord Roger gave a dry laugh. "Carrion crows would have eaten your eyes by now, John, after some royal forester's crossbow brought you down."

John knew the truth of this. But perhaps, he considered, such a death was not the worst fate after all.

"You'll stay with me," said the nobleman. "And have a life of pleasure, John. Silver you cannot imagine, with your poor life." *Pauvre lyf.*

John made an open-handed gesture—what did silver matter? A man was dead, and John had done too little to prevent it.

"You and I can rule the High Way," said Lord Roger. "No proud, wealthy man will be safe from us. No traveler with a fat purse will arrive home with one coin kissing another in his sack. You've always wanted to serve a master of cunning."

John began to grow angry.

"I am a man of my word," continued Red Roger, "and I do not lie to myself. You wanted to be deceived. You're young enough to not know your own nature, but I see it in your eyes—that skill waiting to be trained. I'll make you a master robber, John, a man after my heart. My word on it. You'll be a legend."

John stepped out into the dusk.

"If you flee me, John, I'll have every peasant with an ax putting an edge on it for you," said the nobleman, staying right behind him, stride for stride across the grass. "And every dog with a tooth in his jaw catching your scent."

John kept walking.

Lord Roger's steps whispered through the wet grass, and he seized John's arm.

The youth spun and picked Red Roger up off the ground, holding him high. And threw him down, hard, into the mud.

John found the rutted, hoof-scarred High Way, stretching south toward Nottingham.

It might have been a forest murmur, or John's own imagination—but something like Lord Roger's voice on the wind said, *I'll never forgive you, John.*

I'll run you down.

Chapter 10

$\mathcal{J}$ohn reached the edge of Sherwood Forest.

The High Way ahead coursed through the overhanging oaks. John stopped beside the road, where a field lay half-plowed, under the shadow of the forest growth. A plowman sat in the shade of a hedge. His yoked oxen stared into the distance, chewing in unison. In the distance crows wheeled and quarreled, and John looked long enough to make out the square timbers of a gibbet through the trees, and what he took to be the tar-dark remains of a very old corpse.

He was aware that lawmen might still be seeking a very tall, sandy-haired youth for the death of a knight, and that, between the wrath of Red Roger and the stubbornness of the law, he had no friend under Heaven.

"It's a man who robbed a miller," said the plowman, in response to John's query.

Millers were reputed to be cheaters and, like bakers, had ample ways to skim flour from their customers. In many villages the miller was the richest and least-admired neighbor, but even a notorious miller enjoyed the protection of the law.

"Robbers find the punishment they have earned," said John.

"That's right," said the plowman, without much interest in the matter. He offered John a piece of bread and green cheese, and John accepted gratefully. Perhaps the miller had not recovered from the shock of the crime—the bread was filled with grit, and one piece of gravel the size of a tooth.

John had spent the nights beside ricks of hay and peat, and during one long sunny day he had helped a thatcher comb stones out of a pile of roofing stuff. When offered a night's lodging by the cheerful craftsman, John accepted a new quarterstaff and a slice of cheese instead, and kept moving south, long into dark, away from Red Roger. One day he scythed a path clear of weeds for a farthing. On another he earned an innkeeper's gratitude, and as much thick ale as he could drink, for chopping the hardest and knottiest load of firewood he had ever set ax into, one that had defeated all the local brawn.

Many times he woke to hear hooves on the road, the chink of mail or the sound a hunting lance makes as it spanks the flank of a horse. Night riders were rare because the footing was dangerous, and whenever John asked, he was told the same story: a nobleman was searching for a servant who had won his trust and then fled with the household silver.

When he asked after outlaws along the route, he heard tales—colorful stories and fireside lore—that carried no weight with him. Men did not speak much of Red Roger. They spoke of Robin Hood, as though the outlaw were real. One carter said that John need fear no robber near Nottingham, and the youth could only shake his head, knowing that if he encountered an outlaw—any outlaw—he would beat the man into the earth with his staff.

The plowman let him take a long swallow of ale from a blue earthware jug, and John wiped his mouth on his sleeve and asked, as if the question had no weight, "How far is it to Nottingham?"

"Start walking now, and by midnight you'd see the walls," said the plowman, in a clipped, emphatic speech John found easy enough to follow. "If you stick to the main road."

"Between here and the town is all forest," suggested John.

"Yes, all forest," said the plowman, and added, "but no man leaves the High Way and goes into the woods unless he wants to hang at the end of a rope. It's all king's land here, all the forest, and the harts and the roebuck and the big fallow deer are all his, too."

"I'll stay on the road," said John.

"Only foresters and poachers take the deer paths," said the plowman, pausing meaningfully. "But they are the shortest way."

John did not glance in the direction of the gibbet as he passed it, carrion birds flapping and calling, John, John.

The oaks were church-tall and higher, trees that had never felt the touch of an ax. John could sense the refuge they offered. He kept to the deep-rutted road, though, and when he passed a wagonload of wool cloth, bolts of undyed fabric, he gave the driver a cordial nod and received one in return. The day was sweet.

Until he heard them.

Dogs, baying. Brachet hounds, the sort that cannot wag a tail or lift a leg without giving voice.

John slipped off the High Way and peered back. He could make out three men in new leather armor and a dog-man, an expert handler, with two hunting hounds on leads. They stopped the wagonload of cloth, and one of the carters pointed, his brown hand catching the sunlight filtered through the trees.

He pointed in the direction John had taken. The young giant crouched, still gazing, holding his breath. A rider well behind them, his body shrouded in a long, gray cloak, took a long look into each forest shadow he passed. Even at this distance John could see Red Roger lift his hand to his hood, the far-off scarlet silk sleeve the only brilliance in the greenwood.

John bounded over moss-cloaked fallen trees, half-stumbled over fallen branches, and when he found the long, straight deer path he did not hesitate. He ran hard, deep into the oak wood, unable to hear any sound but the thunder of his own breath.

When he stopped it took a long moment to decide that the dogs were baying still, but far away. John hurried, using the staff to flick a branch out of the way and to keep his balance on this long, winding deer trail. The smell around him was spice and age, years of leaf meal, ancient golden moss.

Tan-brown creatures stirred just beyond the trees. A sapling trembled as a creature wheeled, looking in John's direction. He took a stance, gritting his teeth, ready to swing the staff at whatever crashed through the undergrowth.

Fallow deer jostled one another, heads held high. They were bigger than most deer, fat and slow, the hunter's favorite. Their dark eyes and large ears sought the source of John's voice as he gave a low laugh.

"Sorry to disturb your sleep," he said with a grateful whisper.

One doe lowered her head, and then another. The deer would not be so peaceful, John reasoned, if dogs were anywhere close.

He thanked the deer for helping him, and passed on.

He stopped to listen many times as the golden afternoon light sifted down through the branches. The forest was a place of perfect soundlessness, and yet when a bird broke into song, its music echoed. John tried to convince himself that he was not uneasy about following this wandering path, but he was aware that he was as far from any human dwelling as he had ever been.

"They are the shortest way," the plowman had said. On the way to where? John wondered with a little humor.

Each tree had a different number of branches, a distinctive way of spreading its life toward sun. Each bird made a slightly different cry, and if circumstances forced him to, John felt that he could retrace his steps back to the road.

But there was safety in continuing forward, and so John did—until he heard the music of running water, and stepped into a clearing.

He retreated at once behind a huge oak.

A brook was purling around green stones, too broad to be forded without soaking shoes and leggings. A makeshift bridge stretched across the water—a log with bark worn by weather and crossing footsteps.

John was pleased to see this rude bridge, but it was the first sign of human intent that he had seen in hours and he took a moment before he entered the sunlight. How many years and how many crossings, he wondered, had it taken to tread this log so smooth? What humans lived in this forest, making their homes in this wood?

The afternoon was calm, except for the bickering of birds and the muttering of the water. John made his way into the sunlight, and then he froze, and ducked back toward shelter.

On the far side of the brook, a man in green parted from the trees.

He was dressed like a forester, one of the freemen who tend the king's woods, culling deer and arresting poachers. This man in green surveyed the meadow and the brook, taking a long moment to see who shared this place with him. He smiled, and John took in a long low breath.

The man in green strode easily toward the log bridge. He continued to smile at the sight of John hulking behind the oak. Something about this smile made John step forward and begin to hurry toward the brook.

The stranger wore a buckskin belt and leggings, and he carried a longbow along his back at an angle, a quiver of goose-feather arrows at his hip. John did not like to guess what a weapon like that could do. Even a fighting squire's modest bow could drive a shaft through a man's neck.

On the other hip the stranger wore a horn, the kind hunters used to alert distant companions. The man timed his stride to reach the opposite end of the bridge just as John set one foot on it. John did not like the way this stranger's cap and leggings were too exactly the shade of the greenwood, as though the woodsman had good reason to hide.

The man in green put his hands on his hips and said, "In this forest we make a game of crossing bridges."

John took in the stranger's bright eye, the set of his cap, the sun on his beard, and his smile. "I have no great love of games," said John.

"Then it will be my pleasure to teach you," said the man in green, with what sounded like real zest.

He had the straightforward, friendly tone of a yeoman. Foresters were solitary, hardworking servants to the king, and did not have a reputation for high spirits. This stranger was radiant.

John felt his grip tighten around his staff. "What manner of man are you?" asked John.

"Does it matter to you," the woodsman asked cheerfully in turn, "how men judge my trade?"

John had seen many a market-day encounter turn to fists or even knives. A carefree word, a challenge, and soon someone was beaten senseless. "If you are an outlaw," asserted John deliberately, "it will cost you blood."

John half expected the stranger to protest, or to apologize. But the man in green proceeded farther, and planted both feet midway across the bridge. He tested it with his weight. He was tall enough, and well built enough, to shift the bridge slightly, but no match, John knew, for someone his own size.

"You can call me what you like," said the stranger with a smile. "But I'll be a poor host if I don't make you pay a toll."

John set his staff across his body, holding the weapon well balanced. Before he could advance, the man drew the bow from behind his shoulder.

Then he hesitated. "What sort of game would that be," the stranger asked, "a yew longbow against a span of wood?"

"Cut yourself a staff," said John Little.

Chapter 11

$\mathcal{A}$s John watched from the opposite bank, the woodsman selected a long, stout length of green oak and pared it artfully. He cut off leaf and twig, and quickly shaved the rough bark with his knife's edge. The stranger sighted along the length of the new wood at last, and said, like a man at a craftsman's stall offering a compliment, "This is a lusty staff."

John measured with his eye the strides across the bridge, the stature of his opponent, and felt his mouth go dry. This far from the humblest cottage, no rule of fair combat could be enforced, no witness would protest. A flick of the skinning knife, a quick bend of the longbow the stranger was setting down so carefully on the bank of the brook, and John's life would be lost.

"And tough," added the woodsman, giving his staff a swing. It hummed through the air, a blow that would have killed, thought John, if it had connected with a skull. "Although too green."

John felt all speech evaporate. Why couldn't he have remained with haymakers and learned a simple trade, like carting or herding sheep? He took a stand, midway on the bridge.

"Now," said the stranger with a smile, "we can play."

John knew what was going to happen, but something in him locked his limbs into place as the man in green crossed the bridge at a leisurely pace. He struck John's staff so hard that the bones of John's arms rang.

John feinted, and followed with another false lunge. The man smiled at this, and made an exaggerated feint of his own. John warded off another sharp blow. And then he forced the stranger back, all the way across the bridge, with the cross-body flourish his father had taught him, explaining that even a tanner had to know how to drive away robbers. *Bish-bash-bosh*, it was called, this heavy attack, and John ended the maneuver with a blow to his opponent's head.

The stranger was down, but sprang up again at once, blood starting from under his cap. He drove the butt of his freshly cut staff into John's belly, and the counterattack that followed locked the two, face to face, staff against staff, in the middle of the bridge. John was off-balance as the woodsman stepped back only to strike John again, from above, from below, the wood ringing sharply, echoing from the surrounding oaks.

One blow caught John on the knuckles, weakening his grip. Another drove the air from his body. The stranger's staff dodged and parried. John felt the strength leave his shoulders just as the color left his vision, and all memory of being in any other place fled his soul.

John nearly toppled, but kept his balance. And at that moment, sure that the power of his arms was spent, he struck the woodsman a blow that rang loudly over the chuckling of the water, resounding from the shadows of the woods. The man wheeled, spun his arms, danced for a moment on one leg. And fell hard, into the brook.

John leaned on his quarterstaff. He felt that he would never, as long as he lived, catch his breath again.

The stranger was laughing. John gaped in disbelief as the vanquished man in green smiled up at him.

"Where are you now?" asked John rhetorically, hoping to gauge his opponent's determination. If there was going to be more fighting on this day, John would have to consider his tactics.

"I am in the flood," said the stranger, "floating along with the tide."

He drifted on his back, beaming up at John. This was not self-mockery, not an ironic, bitter jeer at his own defeat. It was not a laugh that threatened worse violence to come. It was lively, careless pleasure in what had just passed, as though the brook, and the bush he seized to pull himself onto the bank, were all, indeed, part of a game.

John kept his staff before him, ready to parry or to strike.

Dripping water on the ground, the man in green unfastened the horn from his belt. He made a point of letting water drain from it. Then he put the horn to his lips and it gave one airy sparrow chirp. He laughed. The second note was fine, a long, sky-reaching sound that echoed from across the brook and from the vaults of the woods.

And then the echoes were not echoes at all, but the actual far-off notes of other horns, answering calls.

John sighed, and in his sweaty weariness knew that when the other outlaws closed in on this bridge they would take his life. He would bruise as many felons as he could, but his days were over.

The stranger asked John what men called him.

"John Little," he said, resigned, but feeling the first stirrings of his returning anger. He would make these outlaws bleed!

The woodsman repeated this name with a thoughtful frown.

"And who have I had the pleasure of fighting this sunny day?" asked John, trying to match his opponent's fine humor, although he had already guessed the stranger's name. When they delve my grave out of the forest floor, John swore in silence, they will not remember me as surly or cursing. I can wear a fine smile too.

"Folk along the High Way," said the man in green, "call me Robin Hood."

John wondered if to die at the hands of a famous outlaw was a better death than to expire in bed under a priest's prayers. John remembered courtesy then, and in the manner of a knight, or a squire well advanced in training, he gave a fighting man's bow.

"I think your name does not suit you," said Robin Hood.

John was about to give a sharp answer, but two men detached from the trees and hurried to Robin Hood's side. From behind, John sensed a soft whisper, a crushed leaf. He turned, and saw a third outlaw standing in the deer path, stringing his bow. Each man was dressed in rough-spun green, with worn leather and use-tarnished buckles. "Who is this?" asked a short, dark outlaw. The young man's words were slightly slurred.

"A man with a strong arm," replied Robin Hood.

"Strong enough," said the outlaw, smiling with toothless gums. "He's cracked your crown."

Robin Hood nodded, laughing silently. Something in his manner began to capture John right then. John took in the way the men looked to Robin Hood for direction—not as servants, but as friends. Curiosity and the bare beginnings of hope kept John from trying to flee these green-clad strangers.

"Shall we give him a drink of water?" asked the young outlaw meaningfully.

Robin Hood smiled and shook his head. "Little John," he said, "is our guest tonight."

Chapter 12

*T*oothless Will Scathlock brought a cup of sweet wine to where John sat. John had kept his calm, marching with these men through the woods as dark gathered. He wanted to learn more about these robbers of song and tale. Now that the fire was stirred and logs split and burning, a fine example of the king's venison sizzled on a massive spit.

This meat was delicious, and John ate his fill, and still there was plenty more. John knew the stories, how Robin Hood would not dine unless he had some rich wayfarer held against his will as a guest. Each victim had to tell a story, or sing a song, and even wealthy Exchequer's men, employed to monitor the royal treasury, were released without a bruise, their purses only somewhat lighter.

John did not believe such tales entirely, and had a lingering suspicion that this evening's entertainment would be the hanging of a tall young man from the north country, his belly full of poached deer.

But among the outlaws was a burgess with an emerald ring and mare-skin leggings. Aware that John was observing him, the man gave a laugh. "I was waylaid yesterday," said the city man, his eyes lit by the campfire. "Robbed and held against my desire," he added with a smile.

"Drink deep," said Will, speaking carefully to make his words clear. "We have several skins of good grape wine, and you know it turns to vinegar in a fortnight."

"What wine merchant's throat did you cut to win this drink?" asked John after a long silence. The wine was warming and sweet, but he did not want to take too much pleasure in it. If he was going to be hanged, he would make his feelings known, and die sober.

Will put a hand to his own throat and gave a cough. "Are folk quick to cut a man's wind where you come from, John?"

"No quicker than in any other town," said John, sorry at the alarm his question seemed to cause Will Scathlock. "But this is not a band of honest men, unless I am mistaken."

"Honest men!" laughed the burgess. "Oh, no, and the saints be thanked. These are outlaws, and the best hosts a traveling merchant could ask."

"These outlaws robbed you," said John. "And yet you celebrate by filling your belly with red wine."

"I have never met a finer band, in castle or in court. I was a tired and hungry man before I met these green-clad men." The merchant struggled to his feet, helped by one of the woodsmen. "But if I don't hurry back to Nottingham this night, the sheriff's men will come hunting."

"Grimes Black, one of my most surefooted men," said Robin Hood, "will lead you to the High Way."

"Did these outlaws leave your purse as big around as ever?" asked John.

The merchant laughed. "No, they took many a fat coin, and I've never spent gold so happily."

The merchant was led away, talking merrily with his outlaw guide.

John considered what he had learned. Were the traveling burgesses of this shire moonstruck, or simple to the point of idiocy?

"Oh, we're wealthy enough, to a man," said Will Scathlock, smiling into the firelight. "The sheriff does not keep such warm company."

"Is this your usual hiding place?" asked John.

"We have no usual place," said Will. "If one corner of the forest does not please us, we seek another."

The fire spat and the meat sizzled. John knew his words were ungrateful, and possibly unwise, but he continued, "Can even a subtle outlaw escape the law forever?"

"I'd not cut a throat to take a swallow of wine with my meat," said Will with passion. "One of the sheriff of Nottingham's men would cut a head off at a stroke, but never me."

John parted his lips to apologize for troubling the young man.

"This mouth of mine was full of teeth," said Will, with strong feeling. "And as fine and white a set of ivory as any archbishop might have in his smile."

To his surprise, John felt protective toward Will, and put a hand reassuringly on the man's arm.

"And what happens to my bite?" Will continued. "In Nottingham, a brace of sheriff's men find me watching a lute player. A merry lute man, who can play 'My Lady Hides Her Treasure' with his eyes closed." Will gazed around at his friends. "A worthy man, by my faith. But I'm interrupted in my pleasure and dragged behind the goat stall, and sheriff's men sit on me, chest and arms, and pincer my teeth out of my head, each one. They had no fair reason, but for the love of their own spite. That right hand to the lord sheriff, a man called Henry, did the deed. He says he'll have the tooth out of every outlaw's head."

"It pains me to hear it," said John earnestly. "I'll beat the heads of the men who did this with my two—" John raised his fists, but then fell silent.

"Tell us a story, John," said Will.

"I have no tales," said John.

"Every traveler tells of ways and folk no other traveler knows," said Will. "It is the price of meat and wine here," he added.

"I have a gift for keeping silent when I should speak," said John, "and speaking when I should close my mouth."

"Sing us a song," said Will, "or tell us a dream, or—"

"I do not dream," said John abruptly. He recalled his dream of the tree woman all too well.

He stared at the men around the fire. *Hang me,* he thought.

And be done with it.

Robin Hood raised a hand, and one of the men slipped away from the fire. John had heard it, too, a deep, earthbound sound, soft but beyond mistaking—something was out there in the darkness.

Each man put his hand on his bow, and even John put his hand on his staff where it lay across his feet.

A guard out in the woods conferred softly with the messenger, and when the man returned he said, "A wild pig hungry, digging up roots."

"A wild sow could tell a story, if we fed her and put a cup in her hand," opined Will, and the men around the fire laughed.

John recognized a rebuke when he heard it.

"Tell us a story," said Robin Hood.

Give me a tale, John breathed to whatever powers listened. A story equal to this warm fire and these welcoming faces.

"There was a woman in the woods," he began, and then he looked away from the fire.

Where did these words come from? What power gave him this speech? John did not trust his tongue. He would not say another word.

He spoke.

"She was driven away by the gossip of her neighbors, and hurt by the lies of men and women both," John continued, without intending to. The men leaned closer to the fire, eyes bright. "She fled into the woods, which had always frightened her."

John told the story of a woman harried by hound and cutthroat, hunter and miller, every hand against her as she fled. He told the tale of a woman feeling her feet spread, green and rooted, and her arms uplifted, forking, her body breaking into leaf. "To this day a man seeking refuge in the woods could climb her unaware, and sleep safely in her arms."

When he was done, John sat in silence.

"Such good company deserves a better story," John said at last, his eyes downcast. A strange feeling warmed him. In some way John could not understand, his companions had drawn this story forth from him. John had never experienced this power to tell a tale so keenly before.

"A finer story I've never heard!" said Will.

"Nor I," said Robin Hood.

That night John woke with a start to the sound of a guard murmuring, Robin Hood whispering, a sound of concern.

John reached and found his staff. These outlaws could not post enough wood-wise guards, John feared. Surely the sheriff, or Lord Roger and his hired swords, had followed him here.

Surely trouble was closing in through the forest.

John rose, staff in hand, and found Robin Hood far from the lingering glow of the embers.

"Will Scathlock went out when the moon rose," said Robin. "To see if he could find us eggs from a rich man's hen-house."

John listened to the night stillness of the forest.

Robin added, "He has been gone too long."

Chapter 13

$\mathcal{G}$rimes Black led the way, and John followed.

The big man had asked for the privilege of repaying Robin Hood's hospitality by helping Grimes find Will, and Robin had agreed. Grimes followed the all-but-invisible traces Will had left on the forest floor: the scant smudge of wet footprint, the subtlest scent of crushed leaf. When the ground was muddy, the surefooted Grimes bounded from the roots of trees, scurrying over logs and fallen branches.

John stayed right behind the woodsman, unable to see more than a shadowy figure ahead. From time to time Grimes looked back, his face pale in the crosshatched moonlight from above, and John whispered reassurance: "I'm still here!"

They knelt at the edge of the woods. A stone wall ran across the pasture, the rocks shining in the light of the moon. The night was lifting and a wind stirred the oaks behind them. The stars to the east were dim, and the first birdsong of the day began somewhere off over a clump of thick-walled houses, the sort of dwellings that might have armed retainers, even a knight and aging squires, men with hungry swords.

A water-well lay before them, a ragged oval half-hidden by nettles. Many farms had old wells, abandoned and forgotten, newer wells closer to home having been dug. While some landowners boarded up these places, weather and time broke down such protection, exposing the shafts to the sky. John knew no one, including himself, who could swim, and to fall into a well was to face all-but-certain death.

John cocked his head, listening.

He put a hand on Grimes's shoulder.

A splashing, quiet but insistent, rose up out of the dark opening in the field.

Dawn edged upward out of the east.

John lay down among the prickly nettles, and when he saw the reflection of the water, far below, he saw something else too.

The dark water tossed. Someone struggled, clinging to the dark side of the well.

"Who is it?" queried Will's voice, shuddering and breathless with the watery chill.

John identified himself, his own name echoing from the well shaft.

"I'm clinging to the moss!" said Will, with something like a chuckle. "I wasn't looking—" he gasped. He forced the words with a terrified laugh. "I wasn't watching where I was going!"

"I'll go find a rope," said Grimes.

John stood. "We don't have time," he said. "Will is close to drowning."

Grimes put out a hand to prevent John from what he was about to do, but John did not hesitate.

"Don't try it!" cried Will from below.

The stinging, bristling leaves of the nettles annoyed John's bare hands where the fringe of vegetation grew over the lip of the well. He lowered himself into the cool darkness, gripping the edge of the opening, where the old stones were loose. Bits crumbled off, raining down into the interior.

John's feet dangled down into the cold welling up from the dark. And little by little he found a toehold in the slick moss, and another farther down, his feet seeking fissures in the stone.

"You'll never make it down here and back," said Will, his voice a sob.

It was too far.

John knew this now, halfway between the increasingly blue oblong of sky and the quaking water below. His fingers were raw from seeking purchase in the cold-greased stones, and his feet slipped and slipped again as he sought the few sure cracks that could support his weight. If he fell into the water he would drown without any doubt, and he might knock Will from his grip on the mossy side, killing both of them.

His breath shuddered, and the sound reverberated in the darkness. Will was quiet now, and when John glanced down he saw the dim figure of the woodsman clinging to the side of the well with one hand, sinking, his fingers fighting, trying to win another grip in the moss. And losing the struggle.

But then John was close enough and was turning, reaching down, one hand gripping a loose root that snaked out of the side of the well, the other reaching down, all the way to the grazing fingertips of the outlaw.

Almost.

John reached down farther, and a cold and shivering grip met his.

Inching upward, the two groped their way toward morning. And at the last, when John could not move his limbs, when his grip on Will was numb, he felt a touch on his hand, a grip on his arm, and Robin Hood was there, helping John and Will into the sunlight.

"Do you risk your life easily, John?" asked Robin Hood with a smile.

John did not know how to put his response into words.

"For my friends," he said at last.

In the weeks and months that followed, the story was told, and each time the well was deeper and Will closer to death. Wine was shared, and the king's venison relished, and Robin Hood laughed the loudest as Will did an exaggeration of his own terror, clinging to the mossy side of a hole.

But more often than not, when one of Robin's men was late returning from a hunt, John was the one to find him, choosing his fellow searchers. When Robin Hood traveled far from the company of his band, he asked John to keep an ear and an eye on the forest.

If a heavy step snapped a branch in the dark in Robin's absence, it became John the men looked to. As seasons passed it was often John who offered reassurance when Robin was off on yet another adventure. John woke often during the dark forest nights, listening, trying to decide if the sheriff's men finally had found them, closing in around the outlaws with drawn swords.

One evening an ivory merchant was captured and led into the heart of the woods. The prisoner laughed with relief when he discovered he was the captive of Robin Hood.

"And you," the thankful merchant said, turning to the giant woodsman, "you must be the other outlaw everyone is talking about. I have even heard of you in songs, unless I'm mistaken."

John had not left the woods for a town or city for so long

that he had forgotten all about market-day rumors and minstrel ballads.

"What sort of song?" asked Robin Hood.

"I have no voice for singing," said the merchant, accepting a cup of red wine. "But the verses tell of Robin Hood and Little John."

"And what else do they say?" asked Robin with a knowing cheerfulness.

The ivory merchant's face fell. "If you'll forgive me," he said.

"Please go on," said Robin Hood, his face bright in the firelight.

"The songs say," offered the merchant in a tone of regret, "that the king's men seek to put your heads on the castle wall."

— Part Two —

THE WHEEL OF HEAVEN

Chapter 14

$\mathcal{I}$t was market day in Nottingham, and the parish was thronged with dairymaids and wagoners, the smell of salt cheese and yeast in the late morning sun.

A pie man had set up his stall in Saint Giles's Lane, and his cry of *"Hotte pyes, hotte"* was drawing a crowd of farmers and their wives, in town for the events of the following day. A dyer's apprentice who had raped a child was to be wheeled the next afternoon—his body broken up by the town's executioner, using the city's venerable wheel.

Farthings tinkled, changing hands.

Margaret Lea turned to her attendant and said, "Buy a fine fish pie for Father."

"None of these pie men roll a decent crust, my lady," said Bridgit. "They use brown flour and rancid lard, or I'm a heathen."

"It would please him very much."

"Your poor, dear father," said Bridgit, "deserves better pies than the leather and whiting-head slabs these men serve up."

In church that morning Margaret had followed the Little

Office of the Blessed Virgin, the prayers Father Joseph had recommended for a bride-to-be. She had added her own prayers for her betrothed, Sir Gilbert, asking Heaven that the distinguished knight might be made kind and merciful. And now, as usual, Margaret and her servant were enjoying a stroll through the busy market.

"I know you'll wring a good pie out of him, Bridgit," said Margaret.

"It will be a challenge, my lady," said Bridgit, "but I'll undertake it to please you."

Bridgit told Ralf the pie man that his pies had forever contained more scales than meat, and she would see the sheriff have him pilloried as a cheat. Sometimes a dishonest hawker of wares was sentenced to a day in the public stocks, if his infractions were extremely minor. Out-and-out thieves were hanged.

"There's not a bone as big as a fly's hair in any of these pies," Ralf protested loudly, so the gathering folk could hear.

"Didn't I choke just a fortnight past," retorted Bridgit, "on a spiny backbone that caught in my throat?" Bridgit was both serious and good-humored. The truth was, Margaret had seen Bridgit crunching up fish heads, fins, and tails when she was hungry.

Ralf stood on his tiptoes and readied a counter to this last assertion, necessary with so many alert faces alive to the entertaining possibilities of a street squabble. "It would take a bone as wide as me," said Ralf, "to choke a good woman like yourself."

A man at Bridgit's elbow made the mistake of laughing. She turned to the grinning laborer. His yellow cap marked him as a hayward—they had to be seen across miles of cropland.

"Is it funny," she said tartly, "the rig-bone of a fish choking me to death?" Bridgit was a squarely built woman with three silver strands in her otherwise red hair. She had been

Margaret's nurse in years past, a guardian of her wardrobe and well-being. She performed similar tasks now that her charge was no longer a girl. Although Margaret treasured Bridgit's companionship, and often fell asleep to the sound of Bridgit singing some enchanting ballad, sometimes her tread was a bit heavy, her speaking voice not as lovely as her songs.

The hayward made an open-handed gesture of apology, careful not to make a sound. Such street bargaining was a form of public sport, along with dogfights, dice play, and the occasional fight between ale-flushed drivers, but something about Bridgit intimidated even the most hale of men.

"Please, good pie man," said Margaret, addressing him first by his trade, which was proper. "Good Ralf, if you please." She used her highest speech. A young woman betrothed to a man like Sir Gilbert was expected to speak well. "We'll take one of your largest pies," she said. "Or maybe two."

"My lady," beamed Ralf. "This pie is the best I've baked in a month, good white flesh, and no fins or scales."

"But more bones than a grave," said Bridgit.

"Ralf is not the pie man who sold us the fish bones," said Margaret, walking slowly so that Bridgit could keep pace as she trudged along with the heavy market basket. They both skirted a dunghill, one of several seeping brown liquid toward the center of the street.

"I know, but it doesn't matter. They are all cheaters, my lady," said Bridgit happily. "Every man who breathes, except your father. And my father, God rest him. And now you've two big pies your father can't afford."

A street pig hurried away from the din of a scuffle, nearly colliding with Bridgit. The big brown-and-white animal made almost-human grunts of apology. The sound of angry voices brought boys skipping down the lane, merchants breaking off conversation to stroll in the direction of a commanding voice shouting, "Hold him, by Jesus, and I'll break him in two."

Margaret knew this voice. She crossed her hands over her breast, as the prioress of Saint Mary's had taught her, to ward off evil.

"When men aren't busy cheating," said Bridgit, "they soil our ears."

Margaret knew what she was about to see—and she did not want to look.

Chapter 15

*J*ust before Goose Gate, with its pretty tower, Sir Gilbert Fortescue had gotten his hands on Osric the juggler and was twisting his arm. The knight's squire and a shield bearer, bald Hal and bearded Lionel, were laughing and cheering as their master put a knee in the juggler's back and forced him down into the street. Sir Gilbert was a broad, ruddy-faced man, who always wore a broadsword with a silver pommel. He pronounced his name *Zheel-bear*, in the manner of the nobility.

Jugglers did more than dazzle the eye with colored wooden balls tossed into the air. They could also make small objects vanish, and sometimes Christian folk did not like the shadow of a juggler to cross their path. But young Osric was admired by many because he was rumored to be a friend of the mysterious Robin Hood of the forest beyond the city, and of Robin's right-hand man, Little John.

Widows and goose girls alike knew all the songs about the outlaws, but no one ever set eyes on them. Margaret believed the two were men of charming legend and nothing more, but sometimes she dreamed of encountering such a forest figure. Were such men dangerous, she wondered, or were they as kind-hearted as market folk believed?

Hal Whitehead and Lionel Ogbert were joining Sir Gilbert in kicking the juggler, and Osric was hurt too badly to protest. Lionel was a ham-fisted, hard-faced man, noted for his tavern brawls and his habit, when he'd drunk enough ale, of settling disputes with a knife.

Margaret would happily have gone deaf rather than hear Osric gasping, unable to beg for his life.

Bridgit strode up to Lionel and seized his ear. The crowd laughed, but a grip like Bridgit's was fierce, and the loud snap of cartilage giving way was accompanied by the bearded shield bearer's grunt as he gritted his teeth to keep from making an unmanly yelp. A few onlookers laughed as Lionel begged, "Leave me an ear, good woman, I pray you."

Sir Gilbert stopped punishing the juggler. He was bleeding and holding his body doubled up on the ground. Gilbert gazed at the young woman he was going to marry in three days, and Margaret looked right back.

"You should be ashamed," said Bridgit. "All of you! And our dear betrothed Margaret on her way home from prayers."

Sir Gilbert was a worthy man, and as a young man had fought in tournaments in London before King Henry and Queen Eleanor. If he decided to punish a juggler for some slight, his betrothed was no one to judge him. She should mouth, "Good day, my lord," and lower her eyes. But she gave him a disapproving look, the sort of gaze the prioress gave a peasant when his pig urinated in the priory garden.

And half the city was watching—thatchers and cordwainers, bakers and fullers, a crowd of faces. The knight frowned, peeved at having his sport interrupted. He gave the shuddering juggler one more great kick and asked Bridgit when she would be done torturing his shield man. Then Sir

Gilbert doffed his cap and made a sweeping gesture with it, doing honor to Margaret before everyone in the street.

The young woman bent her knees and made a show of ladylike obedience that the prioress would have admired. "In gentleness is the lady meek," taught the nun, "and in her meekness beautiful."

"My lord plays a rough game," Margaret said, her eyes downcast, her voice soft.

The juggler was a brown-eyed, bearded man, his close-fitting hood knocked awry. He was breathing hard, and bleeding from his nose.

"An honest game, my lady," said Sir Gilbert. "This juggler's a dirty creature, and should not blemish your sight."

"He made some coin of my lord's vanish?" asked Margaret. Her voice continued to be meek, but her words made the knight keep silent for a long moment.

Sir Gilbert drew close to her and took in a breath. Perhaps, thought Margaret, he would use such speech as he had put into his loving letter, the only written communication she had ever received from anyone in her life.

"My lady will forgive me—" he began. For a moment his eyes were full of gentle feeling. "I pray."

"Kick him again!" called a rough, drunken voice.

Sir Gilbert turned away, self-conscious.

He had a reputation for roughness to maintain. He laughed, easing his belt so that he could give full voice to his good humor. He walked away with his stiff-legged stride and made a mocking yelp, imitating the juggler's pleas. As his squire and shield man chortled, the knight turned and made a handsome bow, smiling at Margaret. The crowd began to disperse, some of the women looking back at the young woman, walking on, and looking back again.

"My gratitude, my lady, for your great mercy," the juggler was saying.

Margaret liked the juggler's bright eyes and ready smile as he climbed to his feet, but she had the positive belief that Osric could steal the words out of her mouth.

"You are covered with mud, Osric," said Bridgit, "and look exactly like the bottom of a shoe."

The juggler made a flourish with one hand, wincing, and a halved silver penny appeared in his palm.

"Good Osric," said Margaret, "you may keep Sir Gilbert's silver." As much as Margaret liked the juggler's smile, she did not trust the art that made solid metal hide up his sleeve, or in some fleshy cranny—who knew where?

"I owe you a debt, my lady," said Osric, continuing to smile. "If ever you need a friend in the forest—"

The forest.

Margaret was surprised at the thrill the words gave her. The woodland nearby was all royal demesne, and most town people thought of it as dangerous wilderness, to be avoided.

The butt end of a spear struck the side of a wine cart abruptly, and a voice ordered it to move on. Henry, chief deputy to the sheriff of Nottingham, strode through the crowd. With a quick bow, the juggler straightened his hood and disappeared through the thronged street.

No juggler under Heaven wanted an encounter with Henry the sheriff's man.

The chief deputy gave a cheerful bow to Margaret and wished her a good day, adding, "There are those like Osric who think there are wonders and powers in the greenwood—and then there are men like me."

"Fat and without grace?" prompted Bridgit.

Chapter 16

I won't marry Sir Gilbert, Father.

Margaret could almost bring herself to say this.

Her father sat on a bench beside a thin fire, holding his hands out to the pale flames, having listened to his daughter's description of the violence against the juggler. He had devoured his portion of fish pie hungrily and exclaimed what an excellent dish it had been, down to the very crust. Hygd, the sole house servant, ate her share with thanks and worked now in the scullery, her slight figure passing back and forth, scrubbing and rearranging pots as though the entire house had to be set in perfect order for the forthcoming marriage to be blessed.

"Margaret, I wish you every happiness under Heaven," said William Lea with a sigh.

He's a cruel man, she wanted to say.

"Knights become rough," her father continued, as though he knew her thoughts. "They live to knock other knights down, in games or in war. His old injury pains him, and a hurt man has a short temper." A horse had tumbled during a legendary tournament in Doncaster, and Sir Gilbert's leg had been broken so badly that now, ten years later, the knight walked with a decided limp. He had donated a life-size silver leg to Saint Alban's in thanks for Heaven's healing. "I know that Sir Gilbert has a sweeter nature in his heart, which a loving wife can discover."

Margaret's two closest friends, Cecilia and Mary, had both been married during the past two years and had moved to large houses in the outlying countryside. Margaret missed the two of them, with their store of merry gossip and warm laughter. But she also felt that Heaven was weaving her closer and closer to the hour of her own marriage, and that this was both inevitable and proper.

She weighed what she should say and at last offered an opinion, with a laugh, as though she only half meant it. "Sir Gilbert looks at me the way Patch looks at a mouse."

Patch was the mouser her father allowed to sleep in his bedchamber. The thick-furred tomcat grew fat on his prey and loved nothing so much as to corner a kitchen mouse and cuff it about for an hour or two, until the rodent was paralyzed.

"The wedding contract was signed all these many months ago," said her father in that tone he used on customers, stewards of the great houses, even the sheriff in his castle, when he reminded them of an unpaid debt for saffron and cinnamon, or even the precious black pepper itself. Marriages were civil contracts—involving money, land, or other valuables—that were solemnly blessed at the church door on the wedding day.

"If I don't receive the wedding payment," her father continued, "my shipload of nutmeg and ginger will sit in a warehouse until rats have eaten it all up." Fighting in foreign lands had disrupted the trade routes, and pirates sacked what armies did not plunder. William's shelves were nearly bare, and there were new shadows in his cheeks. He spoke sometimes of going to the market in London, where rumor had it cloves sat in storage by the ton.

The spicer looked at his daughter with a gentle smile. "I know Sir Gilbert is a hard man."

"He speaks in a honeyed voice when he wants to coax a smile from me."

"What did I tell you—you'll win him to more Christian ways."

Margaret had to turn away to hide her laugh. Her father always won every argument. From beggar to knight-bachelor, no man or woman could keep a surly tone with William Lea.

"Besides," he said, "I have heard that Lionel Ogbert coaxes his master into being faster with his fists than he might otherwise choose to be."

"I have heard the market was all laughter when Osric made an eel disappear."

"I've made a fried eel disappear," said Margaret's father, "with a cup of five-day ale."

"An eel skin stuffed, I believe, and he hides it somewhere in a wink; you can't see him do it."

"Heaven protect us all," said William, "from men without mercy."

"And cruel husbands," offered his daughter.

Sir Gilbert had been married before, to a woman who bore him three infant daughters who each died shortly after birth. Lady Phillipa had died in a fall down Sir Gilbert's stairs some fifteen months before. In Nottingham only wealthy ladies, women of quality, generally married for love, and they were famous mostly in songs and poems. Margaret knew of no such blessed woman personally.

Matthew, the young man she had loved when she was thirteen, had left with local knights to perform duty as a squire in battles in Poitou, Aquitaine, and wherever else a young squire's skills were required. Fighting men were drawn to Jerusalem, where the Holy Cross was threatened by the Infidel, and from which few men-at-arms ever returned.

"I came to love your mother with my whole heart," William was saying, and Margaret was sorry to cause her father's mind to travel this sad, worn path again. Her mother was a colorful, transparent memory. She was like a miracle in a church window, glass and brilliant hues not touchable, separate from this recent existence of meager firewood and patched linen. Her mother had died years ago, with a just-born infant son, who slept with his mother in the churchyard.

"If my husband strikes me, ever, even once," said Margaret, "Bridgit and I shall come home immediately."

"If he hits you—" William looked up from the fire, his eyes bright. "If he so much as pinches you in anger, Margaret, you come home to me, and I'll kick him down his big oak stairs."

This was the side of her father the gentlefolk rarely saw when they stopped by the spicery to compliment him on the fragrance of his shop. Once, in the days when the house had many servants, he had ordered a carver out of the house for kicking a ewer, a lad who carried the basin for washing before meals. The carver had bent his knee in apology, and William had relented, but both the spicer and his daughter were what Bridgit called *styf*: unflinching and, given the right cause, strong.

William was laughing. "But Bridgit will be there before me, all the town knows. She'll break the head of any husband that does you harm."

Chapter 17

"My lady, your husband will be a kind master, by my faith," said Bridgit, brushing Margaret's hair that night. "Your dear father would not arrange a harsh marriage."

Bridgit had a way of patronizing her superiors when they were out of earshot. For years Margaret's father had been "that poor, dear master William," just as Father Joseph was "that dear, kind, squinty-eyed priest."

"Sir Gilbert is a brute," said Margaret. "But with a kind humor he is reluctant to show—don't you think?"

"Listen to the tongue in you," said her attendant, brushing all the harder. "Marrying a rich knight, and all you think about is a juggler's bruises. I think dear Sir Gilbert wanted to have jugglers and such thrown out of the city before your wedding feast, so the town would be a happier place. No baron would have been more thoughtful. The poor man is trying to make you happy."

Margaret saw a small portion of her face in her metal mirror. Her eyes were gray—the color most favored in romances, gray-eyed women awaiting their lovers in flowery bowers. She gave herself another glance and admitted that her eyes were not as gray as she could wish. They were bluish gray, or perhaps not in truth quite gray at all, but common blue, like any hayward's wife. She could slap pink into her cheeks, and keep a gloss in her hair with the help of Bridgit, but she did not know of any art that would change the color of her eyes.

"Do you think I am . . . well-favored?" Margaret asked. *When I am as naked as a needle in the bedchamber, will my husband eye me with pleasure?*

"You are a spotless jewel, my lady," Bridgit protested. "As fair as silver."

Margaret asked for the letter, and her attendant brought it. Margaret had studied Latin with the prioress, a genteel, expensively dressed woman with a reputation for high knowledge. Most women did not read, and Margaret could not read very well, but she recognized the handwriting of the clerk of Saint Alban's. The scribe had no doubt earned a shiny penny writing out Sir Roger's letter to his bride-to-be.

The words were written in dark-brown walnut ink, and the knight's seal marked the bottom, scarred sharply with Sir Gilbert's signet ring. Margaret did not read the words just now—it was enough to have the letter nearby.

"Is it true that the juggler learned his tricks from Robin Hood?" asked Margaret as Bridgit held her fingers to the candlelight.

"Queen of Heaven, who am I to know such things?" said Bridgit. When she was not trying to impress other servants with a court accent, Margaret's attendant used such mild blasphemies—*ma fay, Heuen-Queen.* Bridgit knew all the ballads of Robin Hood and claimed to have seen Little John's footprint on Hob Moor, "so big I went all weak."

But since the marriage contract had been signed, Margaret had noticed a change in the way Bridgit spoke in private, trying out a new accent, her voice slightly more breathy and higher-pitched. A knight was not an earl, but he was a marriage prize nonetheless. William Lea's family had been worshipful burgesses in town for generations, but little more. Sir Gilbert's servants ate fresh bread every day, and Bridgit would join them. She was soon to be a servant in a fine house, and perhaps such servants did not find it proper to speak of outlaws.

At sixteen years of age, Margaret was somewhat old to be marrying such a wealthy man. Most men of name preferred young wives, who would offer more years of childbearing. Most other women were married before their fifteenth year, but William Lea had been patient, allowing Margaret herself to realize that Squire Matthew was lost in battle far away.

"Will you pray with me?" asked Margaret, after Bridgit had satisfied herself that her lady's fingernails were clean.

"As always, my lady," said Bridgit.

"But tonight, I am asking a special boon from Heaven," said Margaret.

"What, my lady?"

"A prayer that my husband might love me as well as he pretends to."

"Heaven above us, my lady is frightened." Bridgit laughed, and gave her charge's hand a nearly painful squeeze. "You aren't the first bride to wonder how the stallion feels to the mare."

She added in a low, loving voice, with no trace of high accent, "All Nottingham knows I won't let him lay a hand on you."

"I am of good fame, and prayerful."
This was how Sir Gilbert's letter began.

Margaret sat alone in the candlelight, the pale ox-wax candle smoking and giving off the smell of old cooking fat.

(83)

Bridgit bustled about the outer chamber, singing a song Margaret half recognized, about the cock between the sticks. It was the description of a child's sport, a trapped rooster suffering stones and thrown sticks until a lucky blow knocked it squawking to the ground. Margaret had no doubt of the song's other, more cheerfully lewd meaning. She smoothed the letter in her hand and parsed out the words.

"With mirth and minstrelsy, before the saints, and meats as you will, I will joy under Heaven with you my good wife."

Margaret had much more to read, and knew it all by heart. But her eye crept back to "meats as you will," the straightforward knight's speech forcing its way past the chaste pieties of the clerk.

It meant more than a happy table with veal and fowl of all sorts. It meant that he would celebrate with her the sitting-down and savoring of this nourishment. It could mean, she convinced herself, that he felt gentle happiness at the thought of her.

"Bridgit, what was Lady Phillipa like?" asked Margaret.

Bridgit came back into the chamber, arranging the pillows and removing a sachet of lavender that sweetened the bed during the day. Her father had been a huntsman, a skilled laborer who beat undergrowth and manned a lance when an aristocrat chose to go hunting. Sometimes Margaret caught Bridgit gazing out over the roofline to the forest as though wishing she had a duty that required a stout voice and a sharp hunting knife. "She was what she seemed, quiet and obedient."

"Did she fall alone, or was someone with her?" asked Margaret.

"The servants say she could not sleep, losing the last little girl, after a week of labor."

Margaret could not say the words that followed out loud, so she whispered them. "She took her own life?"

Bridgit put her hands on her hips. "Everyone knows what happened that night."

Margaret had heard, often. But she needed to hear it yet again.

"She was at the head of the stairs, my lady," said Bridgit, a deliberate weight to her words. "And a devil tripped her."

Never, thought Margaret. *I'll not marry Sir Gilbert.*

Chapter 18

$\mathcal{A}$ll executions, including hangings and wheelings, took place outside the city walls at a place called Lazarfield.

The great field of green grass had once been a dwelling place for poor folk too diseased to be allowed to dwell within the walls. Now a crowd of solemn people gathered, and Margaret joined Bridgit under the sunny sky. Bridgit wore a somber hood, and Margaret likewise—women covered their heads at such events, as though they were in church. Parishioners were expected to attend such executions; it was considered both a civic and religious duty.

The lord sheriff of Nottingham was at the edge of the crowd, seated on a well-muscled palfrey, the gentlest of all varieties of town horse. Only a knight's war-horse was superior, and few would ride a powerful charger in or around a city—they were given to sudden kicks and flashes of strong humor.

The lord sheriff was a tall, thin-faced man who eyed the horizon and the distant treetops and never gazed in the direction of the felon's oxcart. When he passed on his handsome gray horse, men and women gave him the respectful bow he was due. His chief deputy was stout, clean-shaven Henry.

Henry kept his mouth shut around the sheriff, and swaggered through the knots of common folk.

Henry paused beside Margaret and wished her a good day.

"Her ladyship wishes you a good day in return, Henry," said Bridgit.

"A lady-to-be," said Henry, "can still speak for herself." He wore the ebony leather body armor and heavy broadsword of the sheriff's retinue, and he was sweating in the sun. There was much work for such deputies—some said that outlaws owned the king's High Way.

"God's peace to you, good Henry," said Margaret mildly. "You look well enough to defeat a giant this fine day."

This was intended only as the mildest compliment. Margaret preferred to not speak to Rat Henry, as Bridgit called him. William Lea paid Henry a gold mark every Candlemas to ensure that the deputy and his fellow lawmen stood near the spicery on market day, discouraging the idle thieves who liked to catch a pinch of white pepper off the scale and run away. Margaret and her neighbors knew that the lord sheriff would have Henry in chains if he dreamed what bribes his deputy was growing fat on.

"My lady Margaret," said Henry, "does not know what feats a swordsman like me can perform."

"Indeed, she will live without that honor, Henry Ploughman," said Bridgit.

Henry stiffened at the sound of his full name, his father and grandfather having trodden the fields behind yoked oxen. No doubt Henry hoped that some new name would be his: Henry Law, Henry le Strong, Henry de la Dure Main— Henry Hardhand.

Henry readied a remark, but dropped his gaze and gave a quick, respectful bow as the lord sheriff approached.

"Of all liars and thieves," opined Bridgit, "lawmen are the worst."

The executioner of the city was a dark, slight man who went by the name of Nottingham, acting, as he did, with the intent of the entire city in his hands. The ground had been prepared, the earth sloping on all sides down to slats of wood and a small pallet of fresh boards. Margaret watched with the hundreds of quiet people as the criminal was drawn through the city gates in an oxcart.

The sinner sat facing the rear of the cart, his eyes downcast, his hands lashed together. A priest sat beside him. Everything that happened now was part of a formula every onlooker knew well. The criminal was led down from the oxcart, his hands still lashed together, and the crowd stirred to catch sight of his expression.

Nottingham himself untied the criminal's hands, and with the Latin prayers carrying all the way to where Margaret stood, the felon was stripped down to a white linen cloth that covered his most shameful parts. There was a market in the clothing, and every other relic, once belonging to condemned sinners, so the priest made a show of gathering the man's garments and rolling them up tightly, keeping them under his arm as he prayed.

The felon stretched out on the lengths of wood, a board under his ankles and under each wrist. He did not have to be dragged or forced, as sometimes happened.

"He's remaining right worshipful, even now!" exclaimed Bridgit admiringly.

The criminal had been a dyer's man and had spent his days stirring tubs of cloth as it steamed, taking on color. Even now the tips of his fingers were tinged with blue—no amount of washing would clean them. The felon did not struggle and his lips moved, silently echoing the prayers of the priest or offering his own penance to Heaven.

His limbs were staked fully extended, and Nottingham did not have to give a command—the wheelers knew what to do.

The great iron-rimmed wheel was so heavy that four men put their weight to it, rolling it in from the shadow of the walls, through the silent crowd. The men had to brake it with all their effort as the wheel found the slope. The crowd had been silently respectful, but now it grew entirely still. Nottingham motioned, a crook of his forefinger, and the wheel came on fast.

When the iron wheel ran over the felon's legs, the sound of the bones breaking was loud, two reports. The wheel rolled up the opposite slope and gradually stopped. The crowd took in a breath, like one single creature, and waited. What happened now was extremely important, Margaret knew, and meant all the difference between a sacred death and a meaningless, squalid exit from life.

The felon gasped—that was expected, and no reflection on his state of mind or on his awareness of his own wicked nature. His body shivered, and a sheen of sweat instantly silvered his naked flesh. That was all—he made no other sound. He uttered no words except a single, half-barked "*Mea culpa.*"

As the wheelers maneuvered the dully gleaming, iron-shod wheel into position again, the great circle cutting a shallow rut in the ground, the criminal made no complaint. He spoke the common tongue now, begging Heaven's mercy in a tone not of an anguished, injured man, but of a believer in full faith that his suffering would be acknowledged by the angels, and help to cleanse his sin.

Margaret could not watch as the wheel did its work on his forearms. She heard them well, two smaller, less sickening reports, broomsticks snapping. The wheel crushed the felon's thighs and upper arms. The turning, sun-shaped disk that the sweating assistants steered into position was a symbol of the round, wheeling heavens above earth. The frame was adjusted under the criminal's body, and then the wheel broke his back and ribs—and still no curse or even scream assaulted the hush of the crowd. Many knelt in prayer, thankful to see such holy penance, as the wheel continued its relentless route.

"I have been too proud," said Margaret.

"My lady should be very proud, marrying a worthy knight tomorrow," said Bridgit, brushing her charge's hair.

"No, I mean sinfully so." The wheeling had filled her with shame. A wretched sinner had died piously and well, and here she was quailing at the thought of her marriage.

Superbia. Father Joseph had said it crept into every Christian heart. "Some people are even proud of their piety," he had laughed, shaking his head.

The candlewick made a subtle fizzling whisper, the stub burning low. Bridgit had brought this house-made candle from the dining hall, shielding it against drafts with her hand. It was the only illumination in the room. William had met with some burgesses in the shop that afternoon who had gathered with the pretense of wishing a father well on the eve of a wedding. Bridgit did not have to be told that if her master did not purchase a shipment with the silver from the wedding contract he would soon not have a single candle stub to light.

"I have not been obedient, in my heart," said Margaret.

The brush stopped for an instant.

The dark-robed Nottingham had knelt when the wheel's work was done and had slipped a knife through the crushed ribs, into the sinner's heart. The crowd had murmured approvingly at this—many wheel-broken criminals were hung up to die over a period of days.

"I should do as my father wishes," Margaret continued. "And after I am married, what my husband desires will be my wish too."

"This is what we are taught," said Bridgit, the hairbrush

beginning its strokes again. "Although Heaven in its wisdom has never asked me to marry. The men of this kingdom are not upright or warm-livered enough for a woman like myself."

Margaret took Bridgit's hand.

"Oh, my dear, never worry for a moment," said Bridgit, taking her lady in her arms.

"I don't know why I feel so," said Margaret. "Shouldn't I be happy?"

"Why, you are happy, my lady," said Bridgit, blotting Margaret's tears.

Chapter 19

*M*argaret told herself she would never sleep the night before her wedding. Even as a little girl she had known that such a night would be one long vigil.

She did sleep, although badly, waking moment by moment. But each time the dark was perfect outside. She could hear the watchman calling that long, high-voiced syllable that sounded to her like *swell, swell,* as if he were treading the streets imploring the moon to swell and grow round.

"All is well, all is well," he was saying, the words grown smooth over the hundreds of nights of duty. Where did her beloved Matthew's bones lie? she wondered. For all the love she still held for him, his face was blurred now in her memory. She prayed that he might be at peace.

She put her hands to her face, to her hair, wondering how, when she was a wife, this new state would change her nature. She had seen the wives of worthy men, their cool gaze dismissing beggars, no word spoken. Would she be like that, or would she still spare a farthing for the minstrel and a loaf for the blind man at the city gate?

Bridgit swept through the earliest gray dawn, calling sweetly that it was time for the maidens of the kingdom to stir themselves. Margaret knelt, and after her usual morning prayers added a special prayer to Saint Nicholas of Myra, the patron saint of brides. She had rehearsed this prayer for many months.

In this strange body, arms and legs that belonged to her father but were soon to belong to a knight of wide renown, she moved the way a poppet might, a doll given unexpected but uncertain life.

Bridgit gave her watered white wine and wheat bread for breakfast. Margaret dipped the bread in the wine. She could not eat more than a few bites.

"Eat well, my lady," said Bridgit. "This is no day for a weak woman, nor the night to come, either."

Bridgit had arranged for the gown maker and his seamster to be on hand, and the mantler too, as Margaret stood in her father's workshop—the only room in the house large enough to admit such activity. Margaret now believed she knew how a knight must feel as his squire and shield bearer, draping him in chain mail, girdled and strapped him, cinching tight the raiment of battle.

Bridgit gave her anise seeds to chew, "So your wedding breath is sweet." But Margaret knew the woman was simply providing her with something to occupy her tongue and her mind as the apprentices and their masters did their work, deftly, cunningly, full of courtesy and well-wishing.

"Too slow, by my faith, every one of you," said Bridgit.

"I cannot walk or breathe," said Margaret. It was not a complaint—to be so straitened by her layers of clothing was proof of the new station in life she was about to achieve. No new eminence, Margaret had been taught, could be attained without the price of measured suffering.

"A lady can walk encased in stone," said Bridgit.

Margaret directed the mantler to leave them, and she stood arrayed like one of the Holy Virgins of Heaven, she imagined, and felt exactly that far removed from her usual life. Her father's workshop smelled even now of crushed cinnamon bark, powdered mace, and other spices used to flavor wine.

"I knew you would be so," said Bridgit, weeping. "I knew you would be as a queen is, and I am thankful to Heaven I lived to see this day."

The wedding mantle was purest white wool, combed soft, the finest any draper could provide. Margaret wore it through the streets on her way to Saint Alban's, the train carried by women Bridgit had chosen herself, women of "chastity and deep worship."

The street was not paved, and the damp earth, though so crisscrossed with ruts and hooves and footprints that it was flat in most places, was strewn with rushes and white flowers, pale irises, and white rose petals. It was proper that Margaret should keep her eyes downcast, and she did, although sometimes she lifted her chin and took in the brown rooflines and the dark shutters flung wide so that each window could be crowded with faces.

Only before the church itself was there any pavement. The cobbled street there sounded so hard underfoot that footsteps rasped, especially the steps of men, her old neighbors with their ready smiles like strangers.

Chapter 20

*W*eddings were always at the church door, and while occasionally the ceremony was followed by Holy Mass within the sanctuary, in planning the wedding Sir Gilbert had expressed no desire for "any further prayers on the day of my joy."

Today, as Margaret ascended the steps, the familiar church door gleamed, its brass hinges bright in the sunlight. Each step was too high—her knees lacked the vigor to bring her all the way before Father Joseph.

A few heartbeats, a few deep breaths, and the ceremony was underway.

"Till death us depart," vowed Sir Gilbert. He was tall, and with his eyes fixed on Father Joseph he looked both gentle and lit from within by some deep inner emotion. "If Holy Church it will ordain," his vow continued. "And thereto I plight my troth."

Father Joseph smiled, and Margaret's words came from her lips like those of a foreign tongue, unfamiliar but solemn. "For richer or for poorer," she vowed, "in bed and at table."

As they exchanged rings they both gave voice to the further promise, "With my body I thee honor."

At the wedding feast Sir Gilbert was like a man she had never seen before. Margaret had never seen the knight in such blissful cheer or heard him with such a good-natured, beam-ringing laugh. All during the wedding feast she reminded herself that this happy man was her new, Heaven-blessed husband.

Sir Gilbert wore a gown of velvet trimmed with miniver, the fur of a rarely sighted squirrel from the far north that had to be caught, legend held, by white hounds. He kissed every guest, as was proper, and gave each man a squeeze of the arm or a pat on the shoulder. The wedding gifts were plentiful, supervised by Sir Gilbert's servants, who arranged them on a table. An ornamental bridle from the saddler, candleholders, a portrait of Our Lady framed in agate and bloodstone. Otto, moneyer to the king, had given a tall silver ewer that gleamed chief among all the gifts.

Margaret's dowry had been slim, but the treasures she brought with her on marrying were not what tempted this knight, as Bridgit had explained. "Your beauty has run him through," Bridgit had said.

As was proper, her new husband kissed her once again, took her hand, and uttered words of his great love for her with all the guests gazing on. Margaret knew other women had heard such words murmured, but she had never understood what it was like to have the breath on her own ear, the love all hers.

Her gown was decorated with a ring brooch, set with red rubies and ice-blue sapphires, that had belonged to her mother, and her sleeves, with long and sweeping points, reached nearly to the floor. The outer garment she wore, gown and surcoat, was the finest draper's art, silk that rustled when she so much as took a deep breath. Her husband was lifting a cup as she watched, and draining it and looking around, searching for her, finding her with his eyes.

Players made music on reed pipes, a red-faced man playing a recorder and a man with one blind eye fingering a stringed rebec. The melody was punctuated by a drum that had been hung with bells so that it chimed with every beat. Small kettledrums called nakers, hung from a player's wrists, and a small leather-skinned tabor all encouraged dancing. Some of the musicians were attendants at one of the great houses of Nottingham, hired for the wedding feast, and others were wandering folk. "We cannot have too fine a noise," her father had said.

Roebuck venison was served, and fallow deer purchased specially from the royal foresters, and veal, and infant pig and acorn-fed sow and boar spitted and gilded over the fire. Both green wine and red were plentiful, and golden ale brewed by the priory, fresh and not like the everyday brew, which was little better than fermented porridge.

The Heavenly Host knew, as Margaret did then, that ordinary days, with cheese rinds and candle stubs, were all chaff, nothing, to be swept aside. Only such feasts mattered, and a daughter seeing her father—and a bride her new husband—with newborn eyes.

From within herself Margaret cast a vision of joy out onto the people around her. And she did not forget to offer a prayer to Saint Anne, the patron saint of wives who wished to conceive.

That night Margaret bathed.

This was her first visit to the bedchamber that would be hers, and she was hushed by the light of the many beeswax candles, their honey perfume brightening the air. A basin was set on the wooden floor, and house servants poured ewers of steaming water into it, their steps crackling over the alder leaves on the floor. Thin bay leaves and rose petals were sprinkled into the vaporous water under Bridgit's direction.

Bridget was no longer in the girdle and headpiece she had worn during the wedding, and yet she gazed at the servants so imperiously that they lowered their gazes before her and kept silent.

"It will be too hot," said Margaret when they were alone.

Bridgit arranged the wedding finery carefully on a clothes rack as she helped Margaret step out of it, down to her softest linen garments, the ones next to her skin.

"My lady will be pleased to let the water be so warm," she said in her most Parisian-sounding voice.

"Spoken like the cook to the stewing hen," said Margaret in the same accent.

Bridgit smiled, but she did not laugh.

"I won't sit in that," said Margaret.

Chapter 21

*O*ften the newlyweds of Nottingham were cheered by a rowdy congregation of friends, maiden wife and blushing husband both burrowing under sheets to the accompaniment of the ribald songs of their neighbors. But Sir Gilbert kept his guests downstairs and entertained them into the night, the songs and singers well out of Margaret's sight.

Newly washed, and not used to the feeling, Margaret pulled the fine Frankish blankets up to her chin. "I'm sleeping in a room just behind the door at the end of the hall," said Bridgit, with a meaningful glance. She meant both that she was close, if Margaret needed comfort, and also that this house was so grand, it had an upstairs hall that led to so many rooms that one could get lost. The bedchamber itself had an outer room, where the master of the house could admire his appearance in a gilded metal mirror.

Not many dwellings outside the sheriff's castle had staircases, a fact that had been noted in explaining overwrought Phillipa's tumble down the entire flight of broad wooden stairs, cracking her skull. Few men and women were accustomed to treading high stairs.

Margaret was left alone, brilliant candlelight all around.

At the foot of the bed was her walnut-wood marriage chest, full of the treasures she and her father had saved up for years, for the dreamed-of day when she was a wife. She knew the inventory by heart: a bolt of black say, a fine cloth; several ells of *serge de Ghent,* another fine fabric; a fine gold necklace with a pearl full unblemished that had belonged to her mother; and other treasures her father had scarcely been able to afford, including a nest of brass spicer's weights.

Her eyes brimmed with tears as she remembered William's care in helping her assemble these treasures over the years. She loved her father, as she would learn to love her husband.

I am a wife.

At some point in the night the candles burned low. One of them, trapped in a draft through an unseen rent in the house's timbering, guttered and went out. Margaret, feeling already the mistress of her room, if not the entire house, rose and snuffed nearly all the fine candles, leaving only two burning. Celebrants downstairs were dancing to a clapping of hands and a half-shouted, half-sung ballad.

Much whooping and laughter meant that the guests were probably playing a drinking game, perhaps the one that had the would-be champion lying on his back while his friends poured wine into a funnel in his mouth. The sound of cheers from below announced a winner. She recognized the rough voices of Hal and Lionel, joined together in a song about a priest who had to ride a goose across a swollen river. Margaret knew the ballad—it had about twenty verses.

When she woke she was surprised that she had slept at all, and ashamed. The new bride should await the husband—it was something she recalled from one of Father Joseph's homilies, comparing Holy Church to a bride awaiting the bridegroom, steadfast, true.

When she woke again the house was silent. Not perfectly—the rise and fall of quiet snoring echoed faintly throughout the dwelling.

The house remained still until a dull blue seeped through the crack in the window shutters and a bright-voiced bird began to sing.

For a long while Margaret did not give way to any feeling but one of wifely patience. She had heard of wedding parties that went on for days. The bridegroom would be swept along in celebrations that ran to other villages, with cockfights and marathon bouts of wine swilling, while the bride, serene in her chamber, would await her husband at the threshold.

But when the singing bird was joined by another, a woodcock announcing the new day, she did allow herself to feel a dash of curiosity. It was only curiosity, she told herself, nothing more. Certainly she was not impatient—not a bit. Servants would arise soon and begin to mop up the pork bones and venison shanks and spilled wine.

She rose and tiptoed across the chamber. When her toes touched wet on the floor, she gave a sigh of exasperation. A bath was all very well, she wanted to explain to Bridgit, but the spilled bathwater left broad, cold puddles.

One very large puddle stretched from where she stood to the crack under the door.

She knelt and put out one hesitant hand. What she touched was not water. And it was not spilled wine, or urine from a tumbled chamber pot.

It was blood.

Chapter 22

Sir Gilbert was lying on his belly with his arms at his side, his head turned, his eyes open.

He did not breathe. When she spoke into his ear—"*Husband!*"—he made no movement.

A jet-handled knife was buried to the hilt in his back, just below his fine miniver collar. Margaret knelt and told Sir Gilbert that he did not need to fear, that she was here and all injury done to him would be made well.

But even as she said this, she began to pray in her heart for the soul of her departed husband. She wrapped her fingers around the hilt. This was a rare, rich weapon, and one so delightful to the eye that she half believed the wound it made could not be mortal, even as she withdrew it, with effort, and saw the unbleeding, precise hole.

She hurried down the hall.

The house was a choir of snores—deep, sonorous breathing, rasping inhalation. Each door was shut tight, and each portal was identical to all the others. Trapped and friendless,

Margaret nearly fainted, her breath shivering in and out of her body, her hands trembling.

And then she forbade herself to give in to such feelings. She prayed to be strong and full of faith. She hesitated before each door once again, until she came to a door at the end of the hall.

"What have you done?" asked Bridgit. "Margaret, Heaven help us!" She put her hands on Margaret's shoulders, looking into the bride's eyes.

"Sir Gilbert—" Margaret knew that one word, or two, and all harm would be undone, the day made bright and sound again.

"He hurt you and you fought him back," said Bridgit, closing her bedchamber door firmly behind her. She was in her morning robe, a flowing, voluminous garment.

"No, he never came to me—" Margaret allowed herself to see the knife in her hand, the blood on her nightdress. She could not make another sound.

"It cannot be so bad as it appears," said Bridgit.

It is far worse. Margaret could not say this, but willed the words through the dark dawn light, into Bridgit's heart.

"God's teeth," said Bridgit, cursing like a fighting man.

"He is still warm," said Bridgit.

"Sometimes a surgeon shakes a stricken person," said Margaret, her voice barely a whisper, "and the breath awakens in the dying body."

"No shaking will stir Sir Gilbert, my lady."

Margaret wept, trembling so hard she nearly dropped the fine, slender blade in her hands.

Bridgit raised a hand, telling her to hush. She listened, her head to one side. "The house is pork-drunk," she said.

Margaret could barely understand a word Bridgit was saying.

"They are stiff with wine, my lady," said Bridgit.

"Bridgit, awaken the servants."

"We will get into our clothes without a sound."

Margaret steadied her voice. "Have the porter run for the sheriff's men—"

"Hush!"

"A murderer is in the streets," said Margaret, "and we must have him in chains, Bridgit, before he escapes."

"Put down the knife, my lady," said Bridgit.

The thing was sticky. Margaret shuddered—this blood would never wash clean, halfway up her arms.

Bridgit put a firm, dry hand over Margaret's mouth.

"They will think you have killed him, my lady," she said. "Or Henry the deputy will say I have done it. We must speak to your father."

Whenever there was a murder in the kingdom, the local sheriff appointed five knights to investigate the crime and determine the guilty party. There was no other regular means for discovering guilt or innocence. Margaret knew that with so many knights at war in the Holy Land, any person even remotely under suspicion would be wise to seek refuge in a monastery or some other place of sanctuary until the murder could be solved.

Not only should she and Bridgit seek a safe place, but William Lea, too, should be warned. Otherwise a deceitful deputy such as Henry would squeeze money from all of them or, even worse, turn them over to Nottingham's rack until confessions could be tortured loose.

The two women dressed quietly, each in a simple gown and hood. Margaret was obedient under the ministering touch of Bridgit, but burning with questions and trembling.

Dressing took very little time, and then, cocking her head every few moments to listen, Bridgit opened the marriage chest. She rummaged briefly through the contents. Spying the ruby-and-sapphire ring brooch on a side table, she pressed it into Margaret's pouch. Then she led the way out of the chamber and down the stairs.

The dining hall was like a battlefield, the wine-slain sprawled and unmoving. On the benches, on the broad wooden tables, snoring men lay inert and gaping, vomit and spilled wedding wine in the rushes scattered thickly over the floor. A torpid figure had blood on his sleeves—Hal, Margaret thought, or perhaps Lionel. One of the wine-stunned guests was Henry, and he alone was stirring, blinking, trying to lift his head.

Bridgit whispered, "Follow me, my lady, and never make a sound."

It was only as they approached the spicery, the home of Margaret's father, that they began to hear the *chink, chink* of chain mail behind them in the otherwise empty street.

When they turned to look back, there was no one.

Bridgit pounded on the door to the spicery, knelt to squint into the keyhole, and pounded again.

Hygd opened the door just a crack, blinking in the early morning light, and Bridgit thrust her out of the way. "Go rouse your master and tell him your ladyship needs to speak with him."

Hygd gaped.

"This very moment, Hygd," said Bridgit, "if you would be so kind as to move your arms and legs."

"Good Bridgit, my lady—" began Hygd, looking from one to the other.

"Look at poor Hygd, staring around," said Bridgit, trying to soften her impatience. "Hygd, we're not ghosts, we're two living folk—"

"Master William took to horse," said Hygd, "just before the first bird."

"Where did he go?" asked Bridgit, seizing Hygd's shoulder.

Hygd stood straight, bearing the pain of Bridgit's grip. "He said he hired a good horse. And he said, 'Blessings on you, good Hygd. I have lived to be a happy man.' And I heard the hooves as he set forth riding fast."

"Before every baby in a cradle grows a beard," said Bridgit, "tell us where he went."

"On his way to London," Hygd sang out, "to buy spices with the marriage money, I do believe."

A heavy fist pounded on the door.

"Tell whoever it is you've seen no one and heard nothing," said Bridgit.

"Don't open it," said Margaret.

Someone heavy was slamming his weight against the door. Its iron hinges had been smithed down the street by Carr the local anvil master. They were well made, Margaret knew, but never put to such a test.

The door latch snapped, and the door crashed open. Henry, the sheriff's man, fell into the room.

Chapter 23

"Where is your husband, Lady Margaret?" asked Henry, drawing his sword with some effort.

He was still dressed in the finery of the day before, though his rich tunic was wrinkled and stained at the hem. Despite the absence of chain mail, his sword belt was buckled fast, and his broadsword's edge was keen blue in the dawn that lanced through the open door behind him.

"I trust—" began Margaret, crossing her hands on her breast. *That he is with the sacred host who protected him in life.* "He is at peace, wherever he may be."

Bridgit offered, in a tone of unnatural sweetness, "Henry de Law, we have no knowledge of Sir Gilbert as we stand here."

Henry made the sound of laughter. "Ha!" It was not a real laugh, but something at once fierce and uncertain. He made a cut in the air with his sword, not to menace them so much as to reassure himself that he was armed. "I'm drunk."

"Such illness passes," said Bridgit, in a tone of compassionate primness.

"And you think you can stitch me up with words." He leveled the sword at Margaret, and the blade was steady. "I have cause to think that Sir Gilbert's wedding night was less than happy."

"Who told you this, sheriff's man?" said Margaret in her best her-ladyship voice.

"A man of law worth his mutton," said Henry, lowering his sword, "sees who wakes up in the morning, and who does not."

"I wish to speak with the lord sheriff himself," said Margaret.

Henry put the point of his sword on the wooden floor and leaned on the weapon. This was considered swinish manners— the point left a mark in the flooring, and was often dulled by the planks. Further, it mocked the dignity of the weapon.

Patch the mouser sat yawning in the door to the workroom. He scratched himself, and Margaret was caught by the ordinary, everyday sound of the cat washing his paws. She still believed in her heart that one right word to Heaven and the day would begin all over again, all harm vanished.

"Where is your father?" asked Henry.

"He has taken to the road," said Margaret, ignoring Bridgit's urgent gesture.

"So the murderer flies," said Henry.

All three women protested at once, Hygd breaking into tears. Henry sat slowly, lowering himself to a stool. He lifted a hand for silence.

"There has been no murder," said Bridgit, her voice carrying above the others. "You are mad."

"I have spoken badly," he said, leaning his sword against the table. "I spend much time convincing the lord sheriff that

I have the wits of a tame, trustworthy house hound. I play the idiot so well that I forget how to speak." He ran his tongue over his lips. "Of the knight's death there is no doubt."

Margaret parted her lips, but Bridgit silenced her by squeezing her arm. "Not every death is a murder, wise Henry," said Bridgit.

Henry closed his eyes and opened them. "These two eyes have told me that this one is."

"Why would my father kill my—" Margaret could not say *my husband*. She fought to keep from weeping in the presence of this sheriff's brute, but Hygd's sobs were infectious.

"To protect his daughter, some might say, from a knight with a violent humor," offered Henry. He had a field man's accent, but had spent enough time in the castle of the lord sheriff that something of the law's tone had seeped into his speech. And the smile he gave was apologetic, even kind. "I might do the same, if I had a daughter."

"My father is not a killer." But to say it, Margaret realized, sounded almost like a lie, *father* and *killer* alive in the same breath.

Henry belched thoughtfully. "The town saw how angry you were to see your husband-to-be bruising a juggler."

"And the town saw my lady obedient in her wedding mantle," protested Bridgit.

"Maybe Sir Gilbert tried to teach the lady Margaret using his fists and his feet," said Henry, "and the new wife used that pretty black-handled knife when Sir Gilbert turned his back." He pronounced the name *Gill-burt*, rolling the *r*.

Patch padded into the room, pausing when he saw Henry. A street pig snuffled along the lane outside, and put its mobile snout across the threshold. The black-and-white tomcat flicked his tail, and did not move until the pig had sniffed the entryway and wandered off again.

"What do you want from us?" asked Bridgit.

Henry gave a grand sigh. "The lord sheriff is busy with taxes. He judges property, he weighs fishing rights and meets with the Exchequer's man. The lord sheriff does not like to hear of dead bridegrooms."

"Speak plainly," said Bridgit.

"If the lord sheriff hears of a murder, he will give the likely killers to Nottingham, who will use his high skill to tickle the truth from their lips. You, my lady. Your attendant. Your kitchen servant. Your father. Especially your good father, that gentle man. All at the hands of skilled Nottingham. I shall not tell my lord the sheriff of Sir Gilbert's death—for a while."

Henry looked around then, as though someone had uttered his name. "Good ladies," he said. "Have you any morning ale?"

Before Bridgit could move to stop her, Margaret withdrew her mother's brooch from her pouch, and placed it in Henry's hand.

"What is this?" he asked.

"Rubies and sapphires," groaned Bridgit, putting her hands to her head. She would not look at Margaret. "And silver. Beyond price."

"Oh," said Henry.

He let the brooch rest in the flat of his hand.

"In exchange for seeking the rightful killer of my husband, Henry Castle," said Margaret.

Henry frowned deliberately, pinning the ornament to the front of his tunic, forcing the pin through the thick fabric. He nodded, no doubt savoring the thought of this possible name for himself. Henry Stonecastle. Henry Tower.

Margaret could not bear the sight of her mother's brooch as he pulled out his tunic to examine it.

"You will leave us now," said Bridgit.

Henry gave her a look of innocent surprise.

"You may go," said Bridgit.

"The widow of a knight is a wealthy woman," said Henry. Patch approached him experimentally, and the sheriff's man reached down and scratched the cat between the ears. "And fine stones like these will run through her fingers like water."

"We have nothing more to give you," said Margaret.

"I have you, my ladies," said Henry.

Bridgit took a step forward, and Henry's eyes grew small. "I have you in your person, bone and blood."

"Henry Privymouse," said Bridgit carefully, enunciating with high-mannered clarity. "Henry Ratflea."

Henry seized his sword and gave a vicious cut at Patch. The cat tumbled and loosed a full-throated howl. Then he vanished from the room, cat hair drifting down in the light from the open door.

"Poor Henry," said Bridgit. "You have pissed your clothes."

Henry leaned over to examine himself, and Bridgit swung her fist. She caught him on the side of his neck. His knees buckled, and he reached to cling to her as she hit him again. This second blow staggered him, and he lurched against the table, using the heavy sword as a counterbalance to keep from falling. He failed.

Henry was still moving, reaching for a table, groping for his sword, sitting up, grimacing. Margaret ran for a hearth shovel and held it over her head as Hygd hurried for a long yellow cord, stiff and angled from a shipment that had arrived months before.

"My ladies, he is getting up," said Hygd.

He was rising in stages, up on one knee, groaning, faltering, seizing the table edge with one hand.

A step crackled at the door, and the familiar armor of a sheriff's man was in the entryway, the helmet too big, the chain

(111)

mail too short. Henry held up a hand and reached. The sheriff's deputy pulled him to his feet as Margaret kept the shovel cocked.

"Arrest these women," said Henry, sounding almost cheerful, "in the king's name."

Chapter 24

"Sire, it is done," said the newcomer. "These women are as good as lost to sight of man and hen." He helped Henry to a bench along a far wall, where, in more prosperous days, William the spicer's customers would sit talking.

"Man and hen," echoed Henry thickly. He squinted up at the armored man. "I can't recall your name."

"I am new to your service," said the man, gathering the yellow hemp shipping cord from the floor.

"Good lawmen," said Margaret, speaking formally, "let my father's servant, Hygd, and my attendant, Bridgit, go free."

"No, I'll share the chains with you, my lady," protested Hygd.

Bridgit was staring at Henry and the new sheriff's man, rubbing her knuckles where they had collided with Henry's thick neck.

The sheriff's man whipped the cord around Henry's wrists and ankles, looped it around his head, and eased the chief deputy to the floor before the stout man could protest. Then the quick-handed man lifted the helmet from his head and said, "These are bandages, sire, to keep your hurts from bleeding."

"Am I bleeding?" said Henry.

Osric the juggler turned from his work and gave Margaret a bow.

He presented Margaret with her mother's brooch, and she accepted it. It was oily from contact with Henry's hands and from the grime of fat and house smoke that saturated his clothing.

"We must hurry from here, my ladies," Osric said.

"I will wait to speak with the lord sheriff himself," said Margaret, unable to keep her voice from trembling.

Henry had been examining his bindings with a frown. "Wait!" he exclaimed, adding a rude field phrase for the female privy parts. "You *quintes ruwet*," he cried. "You have fastened me up with rope!"

The city was awakening, a goose tethered to a cart hissing as they passed.

Household slops, dumped steaming in the cool, early-summer morning, attracted an ancient sow and her brood. A smith's bellows worked off in the poor district, the sound carrying all the way to this neighborhood of merchants, and the fragrance of new-baked bread filled Coney Lane.

The first householders entered the street, bidding good-day, and Bridgit's cheerful-sounding greeting in return dampened their suspicion at the sight of three cloaked travelers. The tawser at the lane's end said, "Good morning to you, Bridgit and—my lady." No doubt the leather worker could not believe that Margaret hurried along in the wake of her attendant, on this of all mornings.

Don't say a word, Margaret reminded herself. And look no one in the eye.

As they approached the city gates through the early-morning bustle of the street, the juggler bounded ahead, joking with the gatemen.

"Do you trust Osric?" asked Margaret.

"My lady," Bridgit responded, "I fear Henry."

The city was behind them, the road empty. The forest was nearby, but the massive, broad heads of the oaks lifted up out of the shadows, a place entirely foreign to Margaret.

"I'll take you to a place of hiding," said Osric.

A worshipful place? Margaret wanted to ask. A church was considered sanctuary, safe from the fist of the law, but a fugitive seeking refuge in a church could be starved into surrendering by stubborn sheriff's men. An abbey or priory would be ideal, but Margaret knew of no holy site in the woods.

Margaret and Bridgit kept pace with the juggler, a long-legged man. They wore hoods, and looked like three people setting forth on a pilgrimage. Hygd had gone to hide with her brother in a quarter of the city called Smithfield that was given over to laboring folk, smiths' assistants, and charcoal burners.

As they walked, Bridgit reassured Margaret that Hygd could be secret in the poor district of town for years, like a mouse in a timber pile, but that a lady and her hand-servant could not hide there a single morning if there was a reward on their heads.

"There won't be a reward, surely," said Margaret.

"I fear so," said the juggler.

"But we're not outlaws, Osric," said Margaret, the sun warm through her woolen cloak.

"I am called Osric atte Water, my lady," said the juggler. "And I learned my craft in the greenwood. I know where a fugitive is safest—among the tallest oaks."

Margaret heard these words with a thrill, but with a touch of dread as well.

No honest man lived in the forest.

The woods closed in around them, shafts of cold darkness. The huge oaks, and squalling birds.

Margaret wondered again how far this juggler could be trusted. Bridgit was silent, looking back from time to time and then turning around to walk all the faster, forcing Osric to lengthen his already long-legged stride. Margaret had to break into a breathless run to keep up.

"How far is it?" she asked.

Osric and Bridgit strode like monks in a midsummer walking race.

"It is not the distance that matters," said Osric.

Margaret stopped. "I am my father's daughter," she called after them. "An honest woman."

Her two companions kept up their pace, and Bridgit looked back and motioned for her charge to follow.

"I run from no law," said Margaret, words she had learned from her father. "And hide from no man." She was close to tears.

Osric halted and removed his hood, his thin, suntanned face alight with concern. He walked back to stand nearby. "A good woman should never hide, except from harm," he said.

"Why are we going to a place you will not name?" she said.

Bridgit returned to her side and took her hand. "The less we know, my lady, the less we can tell our pursuers if we are caught."

The sound that approached through the forest behind them could not be mistaken: the rhythm of hooves, the musical chiming of chain mail, the crisp sounds of spear shafts jostling against shields.

"We are going to the Trysting Oak," said the juggler.

Margaret had heard of this landmark but thought it was mythical, a meeting tree in a song.

"There," Osric continued, "we have friends."

Margaret felt a giddy sensation fill her, half fear, half wonder.

Horsemen were approaching.

Osric whispered a few words to Bridgit, and the woman nodded. Then he left them, running easily. Margaret felt defenseless without him.

"My lady," said Bridgit, "we must do as the coney before the hounds."

A thicket is no easy place to seek refuge. Hazelwood saplings cracked and wrenched around them, but at last the two women were concealed.

Henry rode into sight on a scarred charger, a horse too veteran to serve a knight, and gouged it with his heels. The horse's flanks were runneled with old spur cuts. "Stick your spear points into the bushes," Henry said. "Prick them and they'll squeal."

Margaret dared to peek out from her hiding place, but she only peered with one eye, as though the sight beam from two open eyes might alert the hunters to their prey. The sheriff's men rode into the recesses of the woods, leather creaking and horses snorting.

Henry lifted a skin of wine to his mouth and drank. It was an effort of some skill, Margaret thought as she watched, to not spill a single squirt of the red liquid.

"You aren't one of those flea wits who believe there are devils and elves in the woods?" asked Henry, turning to a young deputy.

"I know nothing of the woods," the youth replied.

"The forest is a waste," said Henry. "Full of rotten oaks and boggy trails, and nothing else."

Margaret and Bridgit lay still, pressed between the saplings.

The two women held their breath as Henry's war-horse bruised the forest floor nearby with its worn hooves. Henry lanced a berry bush, and leaves and twigs rained down a handsbreadth from Margaret's eyes.

The blue-gray spearhead on its ashwood shaft dug deep into the bark of an oak tree, and Henry's voice high above them was loud. "I was too full of kindness," he said to the horse and to the air around him. "I should have skinned them with my knife."

Chapter 25

*U*ntil that moment Margaret had strained to hold the belief that the law remained her friend.

She thought that if she could stand before the lord sheriff, the law would be logical and full of mercy. But as she listened to Henry cursing, his voice farther and farther away, she felt like the roebuck pursued by hounds, and she knew the dogs were very hungry.

A far cry echoed. "He's running!"

"There—by Jesu!" rang Henry's voice. "There's the juggler—put a lance in him!"

"Heaven help poor Osric," breathed Bridgit, rising from beneath the juggler's cloak.

Margaret added, "Amen."

Osric's instructions had been direct and simple, and the two women followed the deer trail as it wound past the stone shaped like a fat miller, past the tree scored by lighting with a mark like a shepherd's crook, into a clearing.

A grandfather oak lifted branches into sky. Margaret thought for a moment that a green-clad shadow slipped from among the massive roots of the oak where they spread across the ground. But there was no footstep, no welcoming voice, and Margaret was at once convinced that she was mistaken.

A sweet, metallic tone lifted far behind her in the woods. A hunter's horn. The magic of this note made it distinct, and yet so brief it was easy to mistake for an unearthly birdsong, or a trick of her own hearing. Was there an answering note, and yet another slender, breath-quiet answer to that?

But no one approached.

"In the songs, the men in Lincoln green spring with a laugh from the heartwood," said Margaret.

"Spring with a merry laugh, my lady," corrected Bridgit.

They were alone, until the sound of hooves and jingling chain mail began to grow louder through the forest.

Margaret stood *full styf.*

There were no gentle outlaws in the woods, she realized. There never had been. Like the promised joys of a wedding, they were sweet fantasies, airy legends, fit for little children and their nurses.

The sheriff's horsemen closed in, crashing and cursing, losing and finding the trail, growing closer with each heart-beat.

- Part Three -

LITTLE JOHN

Chapter 26

*L*ittle John and Robin Hood stood in the shadow of the trees, watching a cart creak slowly by on the High Way.

It was loaded with flour sacks and made its way through Sherwood Forest, the solid wooden wheels following the ruts in the road. The carter leaned forward, reins in hand, and the driver strode along beside the oxen, snapping a long lash over their file-stubbed horns.

"*Ree,* now," said the driver, using the ancient command to angle the beasts to the right, enabling the team to avoid a great puddle in the road. "*Ree* and steady," said the driver in a calming singsong. Although neither carter nor driver knew they were being watched by two men in green under a spreading ash tree, the two workers spoke just a little too loudly, their laughs too sharp, aware that this part of the forest belonged to men beyond the law. Even though most reports described criminals harmless to common folk, no city dweller was at perfect ease on the tree-dark road.

The two outlaws listened as the sound of the squeaking axle and the groaning ox yoke diminished along with the gentle encouragement of the driver. The sounds were gradually lost in the muted hubbub of birdsong, the croon of doves, and the brash chatter of the wood tit.

Little John heard something far off. He knelt and put his hand on the forest floor.

"Trouble?" asked Robin Hood.

John noted the tone of hopefulness. Robin Hood grew restless without at least some minor adventure each day, and in his boredom he would leave his men and fade off toward the city, or into the countryside with its hamlets and manors.

"One of our men, running hard," John guessed.

The day was about to change for the worse. John could hear it in the sparrows' *chick, chick* as the birds bathed in the road ruts. He could hear it in the all-but-silent padding of the running leather-soled feet. Robin would be pleased, while John himself would be as happy to spend the day sewing the rent in his leggings and keeping the cooking coals aglow.

Grimes Black, the best game stalker of all the men, hurried along the High Way and ducked into the trees.

"A knight-at-arms," panted Grimes, "is on his way."

"We've had a bishop's clerk to dine recently," said Robin with a laugh. "And a castle seneschal, but no worthy knight. John, how long has it been since we had a man-at-arms?"

"What sort of knight?" asked John.

"A foreign knight, in silk and yellow leather," said Grimes. "Armed with a hunting lance. He left the High Way at the Bishop's Cross, and rode into the woods." Most trained men of fighting age had left on King Richard's crusade, leaving England open to the services of a few foreign knights from Savoy, Saxony, and other far-flung countries. These knights had varying reputations, and were considered about as trustworthy as pickpockets.

"A hunting knight!" exclaimed Robin Hood. "We'll have fresh venison tonight."

"And a band of men," said Grimes, "are following behind him."

Robin met John's glance.

"They're armed with spears and shields," Grimes continued. "Riding with muffled hooves, well behind the hunter, a mile or more—we could not stay to count them." Horsemen sometimes wrapped wool or leather padding around their mounts' hooves to silence their approach, a ploy that deceived no observant woodsman.

"Red Roger is among them," suggested Little John.

"It may be so," said Grimes.

In the many seasons since Little John had joined the outlaws of Sherwood Forest, Red Roger had probed the woods once or twice each summer, sending men disguised as rich chamberlains or archbishop's stewards. Once captured by Robin Hood, these men drank and dined like any of Robin's guests, but had to be disarmed sometime after midnight as they crept toward Robin Hood's sleeping place. One recent visitor—a scholarly, well-built man with a rare book of Latin poems—had been intended for Little John himself. John broke the man's arm as he bent to his task just before dawn, a bull skinner's knife in his fist.

The sheriff's men seemed nearly oblivious to Robin Hood's presence in the woods these days. Robin's enemies were the royal foresters, leather-clad men protecting the king's land from poachers, and the outlaw aristocrat from the north, Red Roger. A hereditary lord, Red Roger resented the operation of a more cunning, lighthearted yeoman outlaw, even one some thirty miles away. And the recent attack on Little John was proof that, despite the passage of time, the aristocratic robber had not forgiven John for his sudden and violent departure.

"Let me steal my way to Red Roger," said John earnestly.

"So you can beak his bones?" asked Robin Hood.

"Starting with his skull," John said, smiling grimly. Red Roger would be easy to hunt down—he was a manipulator of men and tirelessly greedy, but he knew next to nothing of the woods.

"We'll make a game of it, John," said Robin Hood cheerfully.

Everything was a game to Robin, thought John. He made a sport of life. Not many seasons ago Robin had brought the sheriff of Nottingham himself, against his will, to dine in the wood. The outlaws still were still abuzz with the memory of this adventure. In John's eyes this was typical of the breathtaking risks Robin lived for.

While John would run with Robin with the last breath in his body, he wished the outlaw leader would stand and fight some day. It would be much less dangerous than this constant dash into the woods, this merry daring, always just barely escaping the sword.

More than that, John wished he could show some manly cunning of his own. Wily poachers, stealthy foresters, and outlaws who turned to smoke before the law were masters in Little John's world. When will I, John wondered, prove as smart as I am strong?

"Let's see what Red Roger has planned for us today," Robin Hood was telling Grimes, and the muscular arrow smith was nodding, happy to hear his master turn threat into sport once more. "We'll study Roger's pretty rules, and beat him at his game."

Again, thought John.

He smiled ruefully. Robin Hood was always running such risks, going off on his own disguised as a tinker, a minstrel, a wandering simpleton. Someday, thought Little John, I'll play a sport of my own making.

Just a quiet, well-knit game.

And finish off Robin Hood's enemies.

Chapter 27

The big hart's coat was wet.

His pace was unsteady, his ebony antlers gleaming. He struggled forward, a long, loping course, up the meadow toward the forest. His breathing was loud, and he was bleeding from a dark gash along his ribs. His forelegs crumpled and he fell, his heavy body crashing into the wet earth.

The beast tried to rise, bellowing windily with the effort.

A horseman burst from a wall of shrubs. He dug his bright spurs into the flanks of the bay horse, the fittings and buckles of his saddle girth and bridle bright in the sunlight. His lance rocked with the steed's steady progress. The hunter's blond leather body armor was spattered with turf as he slowed, turned in his saddle. He looked back and raised one gloved hand.

In his wake a dozen men in leather armor pulled at their reins, scabbards slapping, lances glinting in the sun. A red silk sleeve waved in return, and the armed men spun around and worked their mounts back, downhill into a wall of wind-stunted pines.

The solitary knight corrected the course of his mount with a nudge. The hart was on his feet again, scrambling unsteadily up into the bed of a stream. Again he was down, and as he worked to regain his footing, the horse came on harder, coursing full strength toward the shuddering beast.

The horseman had guessed right. Now he was gaining on his quarry. He crouched low over the horse's mane, the lance locked under his arm. The shadows of the oaks flowed over the horse and rider as the hart leaped a fallen tree. The deer froze, confused, then dodged one way and then another.

A man-shaped shadow stepped from the surrounding oaks and into the sunlight. He was very tall, with sandy hair and a short, sand-colored beard. Little John reached out as the bay horse flung by, and with little apparent effort seized the horse's bridle.

The mount danced, snorting and foaming, kicking at the air. The man-at-arms nearly tumbled, and cursed in a language that was not English.

The rider lashed at the stranger, stabbing with the lance but missing by a wide margin. Little John waited, the bridle in one hand. His companions gathered, until they surrounded the sweating horse. Then Little John plucked the hunting lance from the horseman's grip and broke it across his knee.

The knight drew a broadsword, the blade whispering from its scabbard.

"I'll have you arrested, each one" he said with a distinctly foreign accent. "I have the king's leave to hunt here, outlaws."

Little John took the other man's leg and wrestled him from the saddle. The knight flailed, his broadsword cutting the air. Three men, garbed in oak green and dove gray, were on him, pressing him to the moss.

The suddenly riderless horse rolled his eyes. He tossed his mane and gave a low, thundering neigh. But he did not flee.

One of the green-clad men said through toothless gums, "Be still, my dear," and stroked the horse to soothe him.

Little John waited until his companions had led their guest away. Then he walked to the edge of the clearing and gazed across the green-and-yellow gorse, the wide expanse of flat, breeze-stunted meadow.

He knelt along the trees that love the edge of clearings, the hawthorns and the holly. If a hunter had not already seen the tall man and did not know he was there, he would have been invisible.

A pheasant broke from cover at the edge of the green and flew in a low, urgent arc. Little John waited until the fowl reached the end of its flight, all the way across the clearing.

He put his hand on the ground.

And stayed for a long time, his head cocked, listening.

Chapter 28

$\mathcal{T}$he fire was bright, and the venison turned on its spit. Such game was always best when hung from a tree to age for a few days, but the meat was succulent nonetheless. Slices of it were eaten with fingers, just as in any great house in town; and when anyone wanted more, it was there to be carved, sizzling over the flames.

The knight accepted another cup of wine. "The best I've had in England," he said in his foreign accent.

"It is rare we have a Florentine knight beside our fire," said Robin Hood. This was said in the tone of a lord to a noble guest. "We have had churchmen by the herd, and flocks of merchant-adventurers."

"And a lord mayor with a mermaid's tooth around his neck," said Will Scathlock.

"You will have many other guests here soon, I think," said the knight. "My father is Alesso di Maggi. He is a merchant, and trades in cedarwood and saffron from the east. His son Marco will not be lost forever with a band of outlaws. My friends will look for me."

"They are welcome to find you," said Robin. "If they

arrive, we shall ask them to tell us a fine story too. That's all we ask, worthy knight. You'll pay for your wine with a tale."

"A story?" said the foreigner with polite disbelief. "I am a man of sword and horse, and know nothing of childish things."

Little John stepped before the fire and lifted an ax high.

The sight made Marco di Maggi fall silent. He kept very still until John struck with the ax and shivered a large block of oak. John fed the wood into the fire.

"I know about you, Robin Hood," the knight said. "Men hunt you."

"Men search," corrected Robin. "Will Scathlock sees them coming."

The toothless man laughed at the compliment. "I have the best eyes in the woods," he said to the guest. "A gift from God."

"Men-at-arms, traveling knights—we are warned of this famous outlaw." Marco waggled his finger, the wine and the cordial company making him feel at home. "Some people say you are a short, quick man. Some say you are broad and slow. No one knows what you look like exactly. Are you yellow-haired or bald? Do you have a long beard?" He shrugged. "Everyone says you stand in Sherwood Forest with this giant of a man, this Little John."

Little John sat on his haunches and studied the knight.

"What's wrong, John?" asked Robin Hood.

"This knight has too little coin in his purse," said the big man after a silence.

The Florentine fingered the slack leather bag at his belt. "Times are not easy for a wandering knight. Even I, Marco di Maggi, have to go hungry."

Robin Hood probed the fire with a stick. "Little John has been with me many round seasons now," he said. "Will

Scathlock sees with his eyes, and John sees with—" Robin looked over at his friend and smiled. "He sees."

"I think it unfriendly, the way he looks at me," Marco said, setting down his cup.

"We would not mistreat a guest," said Robin Hood.

"Where are your companions, knight?" asked Little John.

The Florentine rose to his feet, knocking over his cup.

"I am alone," he answered.

"Where are they hiding?" insisted Little John.

"My honor demands I ask your apology," said Marco di Maggi, "if you call me a liar."

None of the men and women sitting around the fire stirred. Will Scathlock poured another cup of wine and offered it up to their guest.

"I will fight you, sword to sword," said the Florentine knight.

"Or match one of John's stories with one of your own," countered Robin.

Marco di Maggi accepted the wine. He gazed around at the curious eyes, and then took his seat again. "It will not be a fair contest," he said.

Two or three voices called out reassurance.

"So this is how you toy with a guest," continued the Florentine, adjusting his belt and its empty scabbard. He looked off into the woods, then smiled, shrugging.

One of the sentries off in the dark gave a whisper, and the small crowd of listeners stirred, hands reaching for staves and longbows. The captive knight's hand paused halfway down his leg.

A burst of wings; whirring, high-pitched flight overhead; and the pale body of a grouse burst across the firelight.

Folk gave quiet, relieved laughs, and the Florentine joined them.

"Pray begin your story," said Robin Hood.

"This story is from my hometown, far away," said Marco di Maggi when silence had returned. "It is called 'The story of the Woman with Two Mouths.' It is a story of a woman with a mouth in her belly." He shrugged apologetically. "It is a story, and it is true, both. She lived in a fine house in Castellina, a town of liars and bandits." He put his head down, and raised it again. "Bandits of no honor," he corrected himself, "unlike this fine band."

The fire flared, and light and shadow chased themselves around the ring of expectant faces.

"This woman was stabbed by accident, in a fight in a wine house," said the knight. "She was so injured, the surgeon offered her soul to Heaven. But she did not die. She lived! But the wound in her belly, here—" He touched his side and paused, listening to the silence of the forest.

"It did not close up," he continued, "and all her life I have been told her sisters and daughters could peer within. They could see the humors moving about, and the blood sinking from her brain to her belly, all scarlet and green. She was known all over the land, and Il Papa, the lord pope, said that someday he would like to see her in her home and bless her insides."

The Florentine took a long drink of wine.

"One day a thief broke into her house, running from the captain of the guard. He carried a pearl in his hand that he stole from a *contessa*. The thief was mad with worry, and behind him were the guards, pounding at the shutters."

The exertion of putting all this into English, or the anxiety that his story might not please, made the knight slump and make a gesture as if to say, It is the best I can do.

"Tell us what happened!" cried a voice.

Marco's eyes brightened, and he offered a polite bow. "The thief was in a panic like this—" The knight made his eyes bulge, and thrust out his tongue momentarily. "He saw the woman in her nightdress, this famous wife and mother. He said, 'Excuse me, good woman, I pray you,' and he thrust the pearl into the side of the woman, all the way in beside her spleen. And his hand stuck! Inside her belly, his hand was sticking."

The knight threw his whole heart into the part now, acting out with theatrical gestures a man with his hand stuck next to a spleen, terrified as the guard broke the shutters. The guard stormed into the room and, the Florentine said, the thief was arrested and taken to the *castello* with his hand still trapped in the woman's interior.

"The greatest surgeon in Firenze was called to assist, and two important doctors visiting from Bologna. They all pulled on a limb, each doctor holding a leg, the surgeon clinging on to the arm that was not stuck, all of them pulling, and pulling—"

The Florentine nodded to himself, as though imagining the scene to his own satisfaction, unable to put it into words.

"What happened?" asked Will Scathlock.

"They pulled." The knight held up both hands. "And when they had the thief all the way pulled out—there was no pearl. The pearl was left in the woman, and there it is still, to this day, giving her good health and good fortune."

Robin Hood laughed.

"That was a good story, knight," he said at last.

Heads nodded, and a voice remarked that a pearl dissolved in wine was the most reliable medicine.

All eyes turned to the big man who sat leaning against a tree.

"It's your turn, John," said Robin Hood.

Chapter 29

John stepped close to the fire, pausing before he spoke. The entire band was alert, awaiting the signal.

The fire spat and whistled, dry pinewood rich with oils. Such a fire was often unwise, the scent of pine smoke alerting royal foresters. Oak wood burned cleanest, but pine was merry. And tonight the outlaws wanted to be found. Despite his misgivings, John saw the point of such fragrant, far-reaching smoke.

Let the hunters, he thought, close in on their quarry.

The wind eased through the branches overhead, and John heard all he needed to know about this knight from Florence: *great danger.*

Where was the knife secreted, John wondered, the one the wind warned him about? Somewhere in the knight's silk garments, or in the leather of his leggings. Will Scathlock and Alan Red, two of Robin Hood's most careful men, had disarmed this man-at-arms, but John knew that neither he nor Robin could turn their backs, even with all these capable hands to protect them both.

Somewhere out there a band of men were hiding, closing in. John was surprised: this time Red Roger had hired masters at their craft—they were almost silent.

Almost.

The seasons with Robin Hood had taught John to use a yew longbow, and while he had not mastered the weapon, he could bring down a hart at one hundred paces, a clean shot through the neck. He could hide his tracks almost as well as Grimes Black, and he could weave a rain shelter from dock leaves and alder as well as any of the others. Robin's band was a collection of poor folk, some driven from their lands by lords eager to turn the fields over to sheep, others fugitives from the sheriff's men—many missing a thumb or an eye, the result of a royal forester's cruelty or a lawman's ugly zeal.

Robin Hood's outlaws waited, cups in their hands, and the Florentine knight sat with his hands clasped.

John wished this life with Robin Hood could go on forever, the willow and the beech their lasting refuge. Robin Hood had taught him to love the very names of the trees, the black poplar and the silver birch, the wych elm and the lime.

"Once a noble lord looked out over green and forest," began John. "And he wanted whatever he saw. Whenever sight flowed from his eyes, he wished sight could cling, and claim, and carry. A cart of minted coin, a wagon of rich fabric—nothing was safe from this nobleman. What hunger is to the harvester, greed was to this proud lord."

Marco di Maggi flicked his hand and looked around: what a weak story this was going to be!

"This lord wanted people," John continued, "as well as gold. When a strong young man came into his sight, the noble wanted that young man's endless loyalty. This lord was subtle, and he was silken in his voice. He could win killers to his art. And one day he sent the young man to the High Way to steal, and the young man's friend was killed, with a spear in his back."

Marco shook his head and folded his arms. He looked at the gathering and raised his eyebrows, as if to say, This is nothing compared to a story about a woman with a door in her gut.

"Now this lord searches the kingdom for rich jewels and new-minted silver, but he hunts above all the young man who would not stay at his side. And he hunts another outlaw, a man who does not steal but gives, putting ale in the cups and venison on the trenchers of the poor. This lord would see the heads of Little John and Robin Hood on pikes. And he will not rest until he does."

John fell silent.

"I win the game," said the knight.

"Our guest wins the storytelling contest," said Robin Hood. "And Little John wins the knife with the crimson handle, the one peeking through the seam in Marco's legging."

"So you treat a guest as a sheriff does," said the knight, tossing his wine into the fire. The red wine steamed as it struck the flames.

"You are among friends," said Robin Hood.

"I challenge you to combat," said the knight. "You, Little John. Steel or staff; it doesn't matter which."

John put up a hand for quiet.

The night birds were hushed. A distant brook ran fast, then altered its course minutely, a footstep parting the water.

"You cannot stay here, Robin Hood," said Marco abruptly. "Men are coming for you, to kill you, every one."

"We know that," said Robin Hood quietly.

"No, you do not understand," said the Florentine, gesturing helplessly, as though English could not communicate the urgency. "You, Robin Hood, and you, Little John," added the knight, in a tone of near sorrow, "are dead men!"

Robin Hood gave the signal then, a low whistle that was answered by a sentry off in the forest, and another farther off.

The hunters carried lances and swords but wore only leather armor—no chain mail. They crawled along the damp ground, hoisting their heavy bodies over tree roots as big around as oxen. Their leader gave a hiss, and pointed silently. Firelight snapped and flickered through the trees ahead— Robin Hood's camp.

Their leather had been oiled so it would not give off the usual creaks and grunts of bull-hide armor, but even so they could not be perfectly quiet. A hilt caught on a sapling, and a puddle gave an oozy, squelching whisper as a knee sank into it.

But these were skilled men, and after every crushed leaf, after every drowsy songbird struggled higher up its hazel branches, the hunters waited, still and patient, for the quiet to resume.

The dark-armored band of hunters reached the place where, if there had been a sentry, he would have been peering, listening. Here were a sentry's footprints, and here a splash of urine on a mossy tree—a sentry had relieved himself. The damp bark was still warm.

The lead hunter rose from his crouch.

They broke through the forest and dashed into the clearing, the snapping bright fire gleaming on their weapons.

No venison roasted on the spit; no blankets were spread. The ground around was scored by feet, but only the blazing fire gave any sign that a camp of any size had been here, and the top layer of wood on this pinewood fire had just been added—it was barely charred.

The hunters knelt, studying the ground. Soon the signs—spilled wine, shivers of kindling—showed how many had eaten here.

"Fifteen," said a voice. "Maybe twenty. Not many more."

The lead hunter slipped the hood from his head, and a flash of a red silk tunic brightened the half-dark. "They are watching us," he whispered. "Even now. I can smell them!"

"My lord," said one of the men, "I think they are far away by now."

"I trusted a Florentine knight," said Red Roger, "to carry out my orders!"

"There's nothing more we can do, my lord," said Lord Roger's man, his voice strained with unease.

A whip-crack projectile flashed through the flames. An arrow instantly buried itself in the side of an oak, its head so firmly in the pith of the tree that the shaft did not tremble.

None of the hunters spoke for a long moment.

"Fifteen or twenty," said Red Roger, his voice taut with feeling. "How many women?"

"My lord," said the man, "we are only seven men, and tired."

"It's a hay cutter's weapon, the longbow," said Lord Roger. "A weapon for cowherders." He said this last loudly, his words echoing faintly through the woods.

But two of his men were fleeing already, into the growing dark.

They were joined by two others, then by all of the men, until Lord Roger was alone.

The nobleman stepped to the arrow imbedded in the oak, and wrenched at it.

He tugged hard.

Chapter 30

"I shall confess to you before you kill me," said the knight, in a tone of jaunty resignation. There was the faintest twinkle in his eye—as though he did not expect violence to follow.

It was morning, and the outlaws had established a new camp. It was the usual loose arrangment: hide canopies, sentries already finished with the first watch, new guards taking their place. A fresh deer carcass was laid out, butchered by Edwy, peering with his one good eye. A brief rain filtered down through the leafy canopy, sparkling in the sun as daylight at last defeated cloud.

Sir Marco had outfitted himself with care, polishing the fine leather armor, the *cuir-bouilli* that was much lighter and stronger than most metal armor. "I was paid in gold coins," said Marco, as though prompted by an inner need to confess. "With more money to follow if we brought back John Little's skin, and Robin Hood's, stretched over a shield."

Little John said nothing. He had crouched in the dark forest under a rowan tree and watched his former master. The sight of Red Roger had chilled him. The lean, monkish face was thinner than ever, and the eyes were fierce. Surely, thought John, Red Roger will never rest until Robin Hood and I are dead.

"I am from nowhere," the knight was saying. "I speak with this accent, it's true, but I win my wages now serving English lords. I care nothing for justice. I fight for whomever hires me."

Robin smiled. "You are a man without law."

"Like you," said Marco. "I know that you will take me into the darkest part of the woods to stick a blade between my ribs. I would do the same."

John did not respond. Robin Hood was waxing his bow-string, and glanced up with a concerned smile. "We treat a guest with honor, man-at-arms."

"You cannot keep stealing from proud, wealthy men," said Marco, "and giving the silver to peasants. It shows a spirit of adventure," said the knight, with an unyielding cheerfulness. "City men dislike it, and true robbers hate it."

Robin Hood laughed.

"What will keep me," queried the knight, "from telling every man I see what Robin Hood looks like, how he lives, how many swords he owns? I will tell them Little John is a great big ox." There was something trusting in his challenging tone, as though in truth he did not fear for his life.

"You tell a worthy story," said Little John. "The woman with a secret mouth." John could not suppress his curiosity. "Was it true?"

The knight gave a quiet laugh. "Little John of the woods. Every traveler is afraid of you, and yet you are caught by a little tale around a fire"

John was annoyed for an instant.

"They'll catch you," said Sir Marco. "The law, or Red Roger and his men—one or the other. As Red Roger will catch me, and bleed me hollow. That is, unless you ask a well-trained man-at-arms to join your band."

Little John and Robin Hood shared a glance.

"A knight will not find enough work among us," said Robin Hood at last, "to keep his sword sharp."

"I will surprise you," said Marco di Maggi, a strain of hope in his voice.

"I have no doubt," said Robin Hood, "that you would surprise all of us—with your stories."

"You will need someone of my fighting craft," said the knight.

John could hear no voice of caution in the birdsong, no murmur of warning in the rustling chestnut tree.

Grimes Black kept three paces back from the knight, his hand on the hilt of his sword. He was the only one of Robin's men who could take the proper stance when an opponent's sword flashed. Grimes was missing one eyebrow, where a sword tip had evidently scored his face years ago, and yet his history was shadowy. During blade practice, Grimes always knocked the weapon from his opponent's grasp. All the other outlaws made do with zeal and arm strength rather than skill, having never studied the weapon in a castle. John's weapon of choice remained the quarterstaff.

Now Grimes spoke up. "My sword against his, for the right to dine with us each night."

"A contest!" exclaimed Robin Hood. "What do you think, John?"

"My opponent," said the Florentine knight, "is not prepared for a joust *à outrance*." Such a joust was a contest that used weapons of war. Men often died at such sport. "I will kill this dark, brave little man."

Every man and woman in the kingdom relished a contest. Two roosters fighting or two hounds, two men wrestling for the title of best in the shire—it didn't matter; any fight drew a crowd. Even the king's law acknowledged trial by combat. Heaven strengthened the arm of the just and weakened the sinews of the sinful.

And so Robin Hood's band formed a ring, clearing a wide space as Grimes Black made passes in the sunlight with his sword, and the knight swung his arms the way a woodcutter does getting ready to wield an ax on a cold morning.

In dismounted battle men usually carried a shield: either a small, round buckler, or an even smaller target shield. The sound associated with such a sword fight was the hammer of sword steel against shield, a steady bang-crash that could go on for a long time, until both combatants were exhausted. This morning a shortage of proper armor required the swordsmen to fight exposed, except for Sir Marco's well-crafted boiled-leather piece and a corresponding battered breastplate on Grimes.

The two men circled each other, holding their swords point down, the weapons almost grazing the ground. Their arms were half-cocked, raised in a habit of defense, as though carrying an invisible buckler.

John held his staff, ready to step in if blood began to flow. The sight of the two feinting, hefting their swords, was enough to give the big man cheer. John believed that good, fair combat made the saints smile, while cowardice and lying pained them.

The knight thrust his sword toward Grimes's armored chest, and the black-haired outlaw knocked the point away. The sound of each blow was sharp, the crash of steel on steel making John blink despite himself.

Grimes attacked, striking hard. He forced the Florentine back, each blow striking sparks in the half-sun, half-shadow among the trees.

A sudden sound from the distance.

Hunting-horn music, two notes.

John stepped between the fighting men, staff upraised, and the two combatants fell back, breathing hard. *"Listen!"*

The sound again, the distant signal horn, the two notes: *Come quickly.*

Robin Hood gave a whistle.

"We'll fight again some other hour," said Grimes Black as Sir Marco gazed about, his lips parted soundlessly.

Men ran off toward the sound of the horn in the distance. Toward the Trysting Oak.

Chapter 31

*T*he two sheriff's deputies confronted Bridgit, one struggling to hold her from behind, the other responding with a cry to yet another blow she struck, his nose bleeding.

Run! said Bridgit with her eyes. *Run, my lady.*

But Margaret stayed where she was. She knew these two men by sight: the older man was Nunna, a hedger by trade, skilled at trimming hazelwood and wild roses into property and parish boundaries. The other was Wynbald, son of a shepherd, a lean, sharp-shouldered lad. In the absence of stouter men, most of them fighting in the Holy Land, such deputies were usually all the sheriff could claim.

"Your hands are dirty, both of you," Bridgit was saying, "and you smell like a stable."

"Forgive me, then," Nunna was saying.

Margaret plunged the end of her staff into Wynbald's ribs, and the bleeding youth fell to one knee. He was up quickly, speaking in farmland dialect, explaining to his companion that he did not need any help. "*She nei is yit bot a littel wee leddy*— She's only a little wee lady."

Good manners and social tradition made Wynbald reluctant to lay a hand on Margaret. But Bridgit was quite another matter. Nunna lifted her off the ground and shook her back and forth, squeezing the air out of her body as she swore by God's teeth and by God's bones.

"Take her down and use your sword," Nunna was saying.

Wynbald opened his hands in apology. He scrambled forward, knocked Margaret's staff to one side, and embraced her. The wiry youth smelled of horse sweat and man sweat, cheese and ale—a fermented, salty funk that radiated from him as he gave Margaret a rough, almost friendly hug.

Still bleeding from his nose, he had the wit or manners to say what Margaret took to mean "Forgive me, lady" as he threw her to the ground. Then the angle of the hilt gave him trouble, as did the weight of the sword when he fought it free of the scabbard. She could see the calculation in his eyes. How much time would he have if he stood, planted his feet squarely, and struck the blow that would take off her head? Would Margaret stay still for all that?

"I'll give you treasure!" said Margaret, scrambling to her feet.

Wynbald kept his hand where it was, around the hilt of his sword, the sun gleaming on his dark leather armor.

"Rich treasure," she added, with her hand on her mother's brooch.

"Nay," argued Nunna, the sweating veteran deputy, his arms locked around Bridgit. He uttered something in country speech that Margaret took to mean "Cut her now." But his voice had a strained, hoarse quality that betrayed a lingering doubt: perhaps cutting off the head of a lady is not the Christian or even manly thing to do.

"Ah, lady," said Wynbald sorrowfully, sniffing.

A sword in the hand of a field man is a clumsy weapon. Wynbald unsheathed his blade and swept his sword up, two handed, the heavy weapon carrying his arms back over his head. And the sword held back, hesitant, unsure of its mission.

The young man shifted his feet, took a new sword stance, and drew a deep breath.

"You cannot do this," said Margaret. "Henry will change his mind and punish you for your stupidity. What does he want with my head? He wants to milk money out of me, week by week."

"Tie her like a goat," commanded Nunna.

Wynbald grinned, a gap-toothed smile that folded his face into vulpine wrinkles. And Margaret knew that despite the awkward courtesy of these two men, their poverty and their fear of Henry made them dangerous.

This time when Wynbald took her arm there was no hesitation. He unwound a leather cord from his belt and, working like a shepherd's son, bound her ankles, tied her wrists, and dumped her heavily onto the leaf meal.

A whip-crack sound punctured the daylight. A flash, and a projectile thrust from the side of the Trysting Oak.

A long, gray-feathered arrow.

Nunna released Bridgit and made a worshipful sign of the cross, dropping to one knee. Wynbald dropped his weapon and likewise sank to the wet soil between the massive roots of the tree.

Green-clad figures surrounded them. Margaret breathed a prayer. As dangerous as these sheriff's oafs had been, they had a predictable station in life, and a bribe, or an appeal to their shame, might still have proven weapon enough.

These new men were out of the greenwood.

Just as the pretty imaginings of her wedding day had soured, so now Margaret would learn the truth about outlaws.

Chapter 32

A giant young man with a quarterstaff stood before Wynbald as Margaret looked on. The young deputy was trembling, and the giant gave him a pat on the back.

Nunna spoke. "We beg humbly your forgiveness, my lords," said the sweating hedger-deputy, resorting to the only high speech he probably knew, the language of city courtesy.

Margaret guessed who this tall young man must be, and she was unwilling to make a sound. She did not even want to shape his name clearly in her mind. She could only watch as the tall man with the sand-yellow hair took Nunna's chin in his hand, the way a man will condescend to a child. Another outlaw cut Margaret's bonds and helped her gently to her feet.

"The deputy sheriff Henry Ploughman is nearby, my lords," said Nunna, speaking his best English. "He is filled with spleen this fine morning."

"He's five bow shots off," said a quick, toothless man. "Not close."

Margaret had heard of Will Scathlock, who was rumored to act as scout for the outlaw band. She hoped to speak to this slight figure—the least violent-looking of the outlaws—when the shadow of the tallest outlaw fell over her, and the words died on her lips.

"Good day," said the big outlaw, the one whose presence most disturbed—and thrilled—Margaret. Not "Good day, my lady." His tone was kind, but direct. He had river-blue eyes—the color of my own, thought Margaret.

Still, she did not speak.

Bridgit was saying, "Get your hands on Henry Ploughman."

The towering outlaw did not respond to Bridgit. Instead he asked Margaret, "Are you hurt?"

Margaret did not answer immediately even now. What, she wondered, is wrong with my good manners? Bridgit was confiding that she herself was indeed hurt, her shoulder and her back, everywhere there was a bone or a joint. "But nothing serious, by my faith."

"I am Margaret Lea," Margaret said at last. "And I am unhurt." Spoken, she thought, like a lady raised on white bread. And she surprised herself again—by bending her knee with a show of castle courtesy.

Was there a trace of a smile—even of shyness—about this lofty outlaw? Until that moment Margaret had half believed this greenwood band would prove even more dangerous than the lawmen. There was no doubt in her mind that this was Little John of legend, and she felt words fail her again.

"Henry's coming," said Will Scathlock.

Little John smiled at Margaret. The tender friendliness of such a dangerous man both thrilled her and froze every thought.

John handed Wynbald his sword. He motioned with his head, and Nunna and Wynbald scrambled, seized their horses' reins, and vanished into the trees.

Robin Hood stood at the edge of the clearing.

Athough no city dweller knew exactly what the outlaw leader looked like, Margaret did not have to be introduced. The way the others deferred to him, falling cheerfully silent in his presence, was indication enough. He leaned on his yew bow, and slipped the bowstring from its notch.

"We are pleased," he said with a smile, "to welcome new guests to our castle."

He sounded like no one Margaret had ever heard. His accent was not that of a nobleman, but neither was it like the matter-of-fact speech of most yeomen.

Margaret could not trust her voice to carry meaning, but she gave what she hoped was a courteous smile. She felt there was something uncanny about the man, his beard golden in the sunlight, his manner quiet. He did not wear a sword, his only weapons a hunting knife, a leather quiver of goose-feathered arrows, and the yew bow described in so many ballads.

"This is a blessed day for us, worthy Robin Hood," said Bridgit, as though she and the outlaw had been neighbors for years. "And good Little John. They say you are always side by side, the two of you. Osric was right and proper to bring us here." Bridgit added in a loud mock whisper, "If you circle out into the woods you can find Henry Piss-bag, the sheriff's man."

Margaret could not believe her ears, appalled at the breezy, confiding tone Bridgit adopted with these outlaws. True, they had the bearing and manners of friendly folk. The spicer's daughter was grateful, and bold enough to feel heartened by the companionship of these green-clad men. But already she was wondering how she would get word to her father.

"Where is Osric?" asked Little John.

Bridgit could tell a good, long story—the sow and the serpent, the maiden and the monk, stories that sometimes made Margaret blush. But now she delivered the morning's tale quickly, looking from Robin Hood to Little John, as though eager to see what they would do.

"If I were an armed man I would nail Henry into a barrel," Bridgit concluded, "and float him downriver."

"If you were an armed woman, no knight would be safe," said Robin Hood with a quiet laugh. His eyes met Little John's, and some unspoken word passed between the two men.

Little John was the outlaw whom boys herding ducks pretended to be, striking at the drakes with their sticks. The actual breathing figure was too impressive to allow Margaret to more than glance in his direction now—a tall, broad-shouldered young man with a horn-handled knife in his belt. From time to time he looked Margaret's way.

"Where will we shelter?" Margaret heard herself ask. She was shocked at her own poor manners. And yet it was a fair question.

"Wherever you please," said Robin Hood.

Someone whispered, tugging her cloak, pulling her into the bushes. It was one of the outlaw women, her eyes alight with concern.

Horse's hooves crashed through the underbrush, bridle fittings jangling. Henry's voice could be heard ringing out, giving an angry command.

The outlaws melted into the woods, and Margaret and Bridgit hurried with them, dodging the outstretched branch, leaping the thornbush, ever deeper into the woods.

Little John took Margaret's arm, easing her over a monstrous, moss-mantled log.

Chapter 33

When Margaret stood in the middle of a camp, fresh firewood stacked in a ring of stones, she had a hopeful, weary feeling that this was the way she would end her days, in this shadowy hiding place.

Little John introduced her to a man in yellow silks and a well-tooled belt, fine leather, tanned so beautifully it was the color of butter. "I am Marco di Maggi, a knight-errant," said the elegant man. He sketched his history briefly, indicating his pleasure at meeting two ladies of the city.

"And are you one of these—?" Margaret began.

"These frightening robbers? Yes," said Sir Marco, with a smile. "I am one of these outlaws, as long as they will have me."

"I think we are safe enough," said Bridgit later, as she brought Margaret a cup of white wine. "But I think we will see no justice, my lady."

"The Florentine knight says no army could seize these

outlaws," said Margaret, marveling at the words as she spoke them. *Army. Outlaws.* It was true that she was further reassured by the company of this obviously well-trained, reliable knight. Sir Marco reminded Margaret of the well-spoken travelers who had visited her father's spicery in the days when business was good. She tasted the wine, and it was the best green Rhenish she had sipped in a long time.

I am here, thought Margaret, beyond all protection of the law, among the king's enemies. And I am not afraid. She wondered at this.

"Knights are very skilled at admiring themselves," said Bridgit. "And so, I begin to think, are outlaws. Not a true fighting man among them."

Margaret found her eyes watching Little John as he passed around the camp, whispering encouragement to a man whose eye had been hurt, and to another who had somehow bruised his nose. John split wood, smiled at a kind word from one of his friends, but Margaret began to wonder that he did not spend just a little more time seeking her opinion on some matter, or asking after her health again, or inquiring how such a mild lady could possibly take her ease on a blanket surrounded by massive oak roots.

She found herself wondering if one of the women whetting arrowheads or tying a hare snare was Little John's wife. Margaret told herself she would not mind if he was married. She was curious, and nothing more.

Margaret stood, the empty wine cup in her hand. The camp had changed. It was more still now, more silent.

Robin Hood was no longer with them.

"Someday Robin will risk too much," whispered Will Scathlock.

John shrugged, a man barely concealing what he really felt.

"Go after him," urged Will.

John made a show of reluctance, pretending he was unworried. But as Margaret looked on she could read what was silently communicated between the two men, and Will's relief when John nodded in agreement.

The big outlaw knelt before Margaret. "You are safe here," he said. "But stay near Lucy, Grimes's wife, if there is trouble, and Will Scathlock too."

"Trouble," echoed Margaret, feeling beyond all fear.

Why, she wondered, was she so sorry to see the towering outlaw leave?

Robin Hood's trail was impossible to trace.

Little John followed it anyway, guessing where his friend had passed. *Here*, a tangle of goat-willow bushes whispered. *This way.*

Hazelwood, guelder rose, and spindle trees—the bare whisper of a trail led through a margin of the woods, where hedge plants married with the forest. Sometimes John felt like taking his friend Robin by the arm and saying outright, "It is a miracle we have not all been killed."

He had often wondered at Robin's faith in the hunting horn. Each of the band's far-flung sentries carried one at his hip, and the high, beautiful note drifting through the oak woodland carried meaning, depending on the pattern of the sounds. John had learned to force a croak from a horn, after hours of practice. It was no easy matter for an excited hunter who had just brought down a buck, or a startled sentry who had just spied a brace of heavily armed foresters, to wet his lips and force from the opening much more than a honk.

But this was Robin Hood's way, to depend on near-reckless cunning, and the nerve and strong lungs of his men.

Little John had once hoped that Robin Hood would develop a more steady, fortified system of communication. But the outlaw leader had clapped John on the back and laughed at such suggestions.

Robin Hood loved disguise and secrecy. Even now he was off alone, without explanation, presumably searching for Osric. "You'll be my eyes in the city," Robin had explained to the eager young juggler in recent weeks. "No harm can come."

Robin Hood had never shared any fragment of his personal history, or recounted even to Little John why he had taken to the greenwood some years ago. Few men and women took much interest in stories of their own childhoods—personal memories were useful only if they improved a skill or taught one how to avoid misfortune.

For all the risks Robin Hood took with his own life, all the sudden flight and lightning rallies, Little John would be nowhere else under Heaven right then but there in the woods—looking for his friend.

Little John felt the first stirrings of real anxiety. Sometimes a green skeleton was found, moss-stained and scattered by wild pigs, a lone hunter who had wandered off the path many summers ago.

A black, stagnant stream reflected a water fly, the blurred wings descending to their own murky reflection.

Every outlaw knew the different degrees of mud, mire being the worst, along with slush, quaggy swamp, clayey muck, and all the other cousins of simple, knee-deep sludge. John crept from tree root to random stone, wondering how Robin could have skimmed over the surface of this mire. Osric's footprints were clear enough, and another faint trace of an instep faded nearby, nearly invisible, evidence that only a practiced eye could make out.

At last John reached a bog, a centuries-old firm, peaty carpet over buried, unsteady wet. Now the ghost of a trail led into the heart of the wood, where it was never day.

These woods were silent.

This was a part of the forest even deer avoided, a tangle of long-fallen trees, skeletal branches aged bone-white. No ax had ever touched this wood, no hunter ever penetrated this cathedral of half-fallen trees kept nearly erect by the crowd of dead companions.

John was grateful for the painful sight—a fly preening on a ruby drop of blood.

Chapter 34

"*O*sric knew he'd be safe in this deadwood," said Robin Hood.

"And he is," said John, with forced heartiness. "A meadow mouse couldn't trace his steps."

Osric put out a hand, and John took it. It was cold, and clotted with dried blood.

"I knew you'd find me," said the juggler, his voice faint and broken.

A flap of scalp hung down over his ear, and blood had soaked into his cloak, more blood than John had thought possible.

"A spear," said Robin Hood.

"Thrown by a strong arm," whispered Osric. One corner of his mouth hitched upward in an attempted smile.

"From behind," said Little John.

"I am no fighting man," laughed Osric weakly.

"And no coward," said John.

Many seasons ago Robin Hood had shown Osric, son of a quarryman, how to let his natural nimbleness develop, how to hide farthings while showing off empty hands, and how to keep five blunt knives in the air at once. Osric's trick with a stuffed eel was John's favorite, the leathery eel rolling up tight under the juggler's arm and then leaping out to startle and delight both children and their parents.

"I have so much to tell you both," said Osric.

Robin Hood gently, and very slowly, lifted the scarlet flap of scalp—and hesitated. "We hear nothing but stories, Little John and I," he said. "We both tire of travelers' tales." Robin's face was pale.

The outlaw leader gently pressed the flap of skin against the red skull wound. Osric shuddered and fainted, his hand falling to his breast.

"They say red wine fills a bled-out body with new blood," offered Little John. "We have fat wineskins, both rowan wine and grape."

Robin Hood stood. "I taught Osric to trust his hands."

"And you taught him well."

"I taught him *trust*."

For an instant John recalled his own father, who had traveled to Whitby and bought green hides, so rank the new hides crawled with maggots. "Wash them in the sea," his father had told John. In the cold salt waves.

"I know what to do," said John.

He knelt and gathered the juggler into his arms. John could not stand upright in this low tangle of dead branches.

Osric murmured, "Of course you do."

John wanted to laugh, despite his friend's torment. "Osric, you pretend to make coins invisible; you pretend to faint; you pretend to bleed."

"I'll pretend to die," said Osric.

The wound began to ooze as John carried the juggler through the moon-pale woods. He prayed to the hosts of

Heaven, and to the powers of the greenwood, as the living trees closed around the three men.

"I'll need salt and water," said John.

"I'll bring you an ocean, John," said Robin Hood.

"I'm a tanner's son," said John. "A man's skin is but a hide."

"All the oceans of the world," said Robin, "are yours."

And so Robin Hood left John again, with Osric in John's arms. John prayed that he could find the way, and that Henry was not lancing through the woods with a new score of men.

By the time Little John brought Osric into camp, it was dark. Salt of every variety sat around in the firelight, bags of glinting white spread open, copper bowls and leather pails brimmed full. A large lick of salt, worn by the tongues of cattle, was in Edwy's hands. As he shaved the salt with a small knife into a pot of simmering water, he peered up with his one good eye and said, "As salt as any sea, John."

Little John borrowed a needle from Carl Taw, who had been a glover's apprentice until his master had choked on a bacon rind and deputies tried to extort coins from Carl, accusing him of murder.

John waited until Osric had swallowed his fill of an entire skin of wine, dark and red. Then, with Osric singing the song of the cook and the cockerel, John cradled the wounded head and, in the firelight, washed the exposed injury with salt water.

"It doesn't hurt!" marveled Osric at first. He continued the song, about a roast bird that protested at the touch of the carving knife, stood up, and scolded the entire table for gluttony.

"I joy to hear it does not pain you," said John.

Then, "It smarts, but does not sting." Another verse of

the song, the tune weak but steady, the roast fowl running, pursued by amazed dogs and cats.

"I pray it's so," said John.

Then Osric, sweating and trembling, did not speak.

John sewed the scalp as his father used to mend a ragged hide. Some said that green leather would heal, like living flesh, if the tanner's stitch was smart.

John knew only that stitching this living skin was nothing he was prepared to do, even as he did it, praying under his breath for steadiness of hand and clarity of sight. And he was aware, too, of a step, and a figure kneeling beside him.

Margaret took Osric's hand. "Brave juggler," she said quietly.

John did not know why he gave so much thought to the way her hair hung over one shoulder.

"My lady," gasped Osric, and when he fainted this time he did not wake for hours.

Chapter 35

As Osric slept, Margaret told Little John and Robin Hood of her fears. The other outlaws listened too.

She explained the necessity of getting word to her father to stay away from Nottingham. The law was swift but inaccurate, and Margaret had heard that out of every hundred killers, only one was ever justly punished. She wondered, too, how many of the souls punished for their crimes were in truth guilty. Her father had explained to her once that sometimes it did not matter—the body on the gibbet was warning to future felons. Henry would be waiting all the while for Margaret or her father to slip into his grasp, and he would extort as much gold from them as he could.

Why did Sir Marco smile so brightly? Margaret wondered. He had an accent that told of far-flung places, courts of high honor. There was a radiant, worldly quality about him that won her trust. Bridgit, however, sat with folded arms, and when the Florentine spoke she gave him a long sideways glance.

"The road is not fit for honest travelers like William Lea," said Little John. "Henry may well send a few deputies after him and bring him back like a prize ram."

"I will find him first," said Marco. And when no one spoke, he added, "I'll go and stay with him as he does his business in London, and keep him safely away from Nottingham."

"Oh, please do!" exclaimed Margaret.

Robin Hood turned to Little John. His tone was light, nearly ironic, but his phrasing serious. "What say you, John?"

Margaret wondered if she had made a blunder, and the figures around the fire were silent.

A muscular man with black hair cut off short around his head said, "Our contest was never finished."

Margaret studied the bright faces ringing the firelight. She understood now that she had made a mistake in eagerly agreeing to the knight's suggestion—there was something between this knight and the rest of the band.

"I am ready," said Marco. "To fight, or to ride."

John reached for a stick that jutted out from the fire and held up the blazing kindling, examining the sputtering flame. He turned his head, as though listening to the whisper of the fire, and no one made a sound. Then he thrust the stick back into the fire. "Some say the word of a prince," he said, "is stronger than the oath of a harvester."

The knight made an open-handed gesture—what was John trying to say?

The tall outlaw continued, "I think a word between friends is equal to a king's oath."

The Florentine had appeared ready to dispute whatever was said, but at John's words his features softened. He looked down into the fire. "You remind me that I am a man of honor," he said.

"And a friend," added Little John.

"Not yet a friend, I fear," Marco corrected him, "until I win your trust."

Robin Hood smiled. "Little John sees into your heart, knight."

"Then he sees a man," said the Florentine, "who hires his sword to any lord with gold, and a dangerous enemy."

Margaret sought the words to protest—this was not the man who should ride off after her father. But the knight was already asking for the help of the folk around the firelight, and the black-haired man came to his aid, helping the knight strap on a boiled-leather chest piece. The young man with the squinting eye led a charger near to the fire, and Marco spent a long time adjusting straps, cinching leather.

Little John helped him into the saddle, and the knight's silks were brilliant in the firelight.

"I swear," said Marco firmly, "that I will give my life to protect William Lea. Upon my honor."

He said this to Little John, the fire alive in his eyes. Then Will Scathlock laughingly remarked that Marco would ride off into the embrace of the nearest tree if he was not shown the way.

Grimes Black soothed the charger, leading the horse along a path that had to be followed by memory—the starlight was not bright enough, and the moon had not risen.

Osric opened his eyes.

An owl skimmed the darkness over the smoldering fire.

Little John offered him a cup of wine. "Good red sweet wine," he said, "the gift of a castle seneschal not one week ago."

Margaret soothed the juggler's face with a wet cloth.

Osric tried to indicate with his smile that he was reassured, but his lips were stiff and his tongue unsteady. "The sheriff's deputies are angry."

"Aren't they always displeased about something?" asked John.

"Henry and his hirelings want Robin Hood's head," said Osric.

The big outlaw sensed even worse trouble. Since his forced visit to the greenwood, the lord sheriff had seemed to tolerate Robin and his band—although the lawman's deputies had been a source of concern. John had always believed that the sheriff himself would eventually be forced once again to resume the persecution that would bring down the outlaw and all his friends. John had dreamed of a few more months of this, a year or two of freedom. He had prayed for it—knowing all the while that it couldn't last.

"We have always lived with danger," John offered with a feigned carelessness.

"We will not be safe here," said Osric in a steel whisper that chilled John.

Osric put a weak hand on Little John's sleeve and added, "The day is near when our story is done."

Chapter 36

*L*ittle John led the way, early morning light lifting a mist out of the woodland, Margaret and Bridgit following.

In the wake of Osric's warning, Robin and John had agreed that Margaret and her servant should go to a place far out of danger. Although she was reluctant to leave their company, Margaret felt the shift in the band's mood, the way laughs were forced, and the whetstones brought out to whisper against knives.

Now deer browsed in the low-hanging branches among the rough-hewn stumps of oaks. The king's men had sold wood to lords building manor houses, the giant oaks contributing their branches to the barons' drinking halls. The occasional scattering of dew raining down from the trees beaded on Margaret's cloak.

She knew that she was unthinkably far from home. They were perhaps three hours' walk from Nottingham—if either she or Bridgit had been able to follow such a bare wrinkle of a trail. They had left Osric sleeping, sweating with a light fever, and as Margaret followed her lofty friend, she breathed a prayer to Saint Bride, who watched over every Christian's health.

When Margaret asked where they were going, John seemed surprised, as though he expected her to know without being told. "We have a sanctuary for you in the village of Blackwell."

This news gave her no joy. Margaret had heard of Blackwell. It was a village where, as rumor had it, a stray pig had recently killed and eaten an infant boy—Nottingham folk could talk of nothing else. Pigs were dangerous to swaddled infants in every town, but Blackwell was Pigwell, as far as Nottingham was concerned.

The old sow even ate the toenails—that's what Margaret had heard.

"You take us to a village," said Bridgit, "no citizen of Nottingham would send a dung fly to live in."

John gave a gentle laugh, but persisted in leading them on. He guided them along a boggy stretch of the woods, the earth here flat brown peat and stunted grasses. The earth was spongy underfoot, the ancient bog dry only on the surface. The trees here were slim, and not tall, but their writhing, gnarled branches made Margaret believe they were centuries old.

Their footsteps made little noise, but neither did the step of an armed man who appeared suddenly across the brown blanket of bog land.

John froze.

The stranger stepped from a thicket of willows.

He was dressed like one of the outlaws. But then the dark, fine leather of his belt, and the new leather of his quiver, and his high ox-hide leggings, barely scarred with brambles, made him look like another sort of man entirely. He carried a cross-bow and wore a short sword.

He was standing erect and still, and Little John took one pace from the path and leaned on his staff.

The two men eyed each other, a stone's throw apart. The stranger made a point of adjusting his belt, as though he had no greater concern than the fit of his equipment. He slipped a bolt from the quiver at his hip.

"Take three strides off the trail, both of you," whispered Little John. "Margaret, put your hand into your mantle, like you're reaching for a weapon."

A long, sunny moment, the bog land golden in the sunlight. Margaret reached into her mantle, surprised at how it felt to stand like a woman braced to withdraw a heavy blade. It gave her an odd pleasure. She waited like someone accustomed to such danger, although her heart hammered.

After an endless moment, the stranger turned. Without any nod or gesture, he melted into the stunted woods.

"A royal forester," said John, answering Margaret's query. "He protects the king's land from poachers."

"Is he—" She did not know how to phrase the question politely. "Is he an enemy of ours?" Ours. She was surprised at her choice of words.

"Indeed he is," said John. "But alone like that he is out-numbered."

"Surely he sees that Bridgit and I are—"

"Outlaw women," said John. "He has good reason to be afraid."

Later, as the trees closed in again, John held up a hand.

He knelt and, using his staff, lifted a screen of alder branches from the ground. The artfully arranged branches shed leaf mold and twigs as the big outlaw lifted the cover like the giant page of a book. The exposed pit was deep. Sharpened stakes gleamed at the bottom, thrusting up out of the shadows.

"The royal foresters set two kinds of mantrap," John explained. "One is a snare, with a noose that closes around your foot and leaves you dangling. And there is this sort, a hole with ash-wood stakes."

The sight gave Margaret a dull, sick feeling.

"Never," cautioned Little John, "try to find your way alone."

As they left the woods, a peasant gathering firewood was reaching up into a tree to disentangle a dead branch that had fallen only partway. Margaret was relieved to see that such customs continued even so far away from Nottingham: peasants were allowed to gather firewood from the ground, and from living trees, but only by hook or crook. Cutting wood from a living tree was a crime.

The village they reached at last was a scattered assortment of cottages, cooking smoke shrouding the dark fields, the clouds hovering low, nearly to the treetops. The houses were pale under dark thatch. In most villages near Nottingham, many of the buildings were decayed, the wattle and daub collapsed, doves nesting in the ruins. But the cottages here were well kept. A house cat sat on a high doorsill, licking its whiskers as they passed.

John stopped and gave a great sigh. "I thought we would have better luck today," he said.

A ram lifted his head from behind a wall, showing off his set of curved, flint-gray horns. Villages often let a ram or even a bull roam free, servicing the breeding livestock and, incidentally, guarding the village from strangers.

"It's Old Fred," said Little John.

"I've never," said Bridgit with a laugh, "heard of an outlaw afraid of a sheep."

The ram bounded over the stone wall and rushed down toward them, lowering his head. The attack was so direct and without warning that it would have been comical if it had not been so fast. The armored head of this woolly projectile was directed right at Bridgit.

The attendant set her staff firmly in the ground, moving like a woman of wide experience, and the ram ran into it with a great *thwack*. He bounced back, but did not fall. At once Bridgit brandished her staff, driving the animal to one side and sending the scrambling, determined creature in a wide circle, right at Margaret.

Margaret's staff struck the ram a ringing blow exactly between the horns. The sound of the impact was startling and buckled the beast's forelegs. But the ram knocked Margaret down, driving much of the air from her body. His unthinking eyes looked through Margaret, beyond her, intent on colliding with anything on earth that challenged him.

John drove his staff into the ram's side, and the animal tumbled, rolling across an expanse of cow manure and sloppy mud. No livestock were in sight, but manure was wetly slathered all over the path, halfway up the stone wall. The ram came on again, and John used an economical, even gentle check against this new attack, driving the beast back, and back again, without hitting the animal anywhere but on his armored head.

At last Old Fred set his feet. He lowered his horns, but did not try again.

John offered Margaret his hand, and she took it, climbing to her feet. Laughingly, she reassured her two companions that she was quite well.

She thanked John.

It was a simple statement, her blue eyes on his. "I thank you, John."

But he would repeat the words in his mind over the days to come, giving them special weight.

Chapter 37

The priory of Saint Agnes boasted only one nun, a red-cheeked, briskly cordial prioress. She bid them all good day and set fresh ale and a large, round loaf of warm, cream-white bread on the table before them. If there were any servants, Margaret did not see them.

"Did that old ram bother you?" asked Sister Barbara.

"Some of us more than others," sniffed Bridgit, breaking off a piece of bread and eyeing it carefully.

John had left them and, in Margaret's eyes, without his presence the rooms were both empty and colorless. Before he left, Sister Barbara had given him a palfrey, a mild, cream-pale horse. "I ride a horse worse than any fisher's wife," said John with a laugh.

"Robin Hood will find use for a mount like this," said the prioress. The name of the outlaw was uttered almost soundlessly, an incantation it was unwise to overuse.

A lime wash had been used to cover every inch of every wall, and fresh, amber-bright rushes covered the earthen floor. This was as clean and pleasant as a room could be, and without a single old bone or bread crust visible on the floor, as was usual even in holy dwellings. But Margaret found herself wishing that John was sitting there at the table, smiling patiently at Bridgit's tart "One of us let the old ram attack two women before he stirred his stick."

"Old Fred should work for the sheriff," said Margaret.

"That sheep is much too smart to be a deputy, my lady," said Bridgit.

The stone buildings of this holy place were set well away from the village of Blackwell. From the kitchen where they sat, it had a good view of anyone who walked the paths that crisscrossed the village green. Flowers beside the cottages were bright, yellow daisies and flowering herbs, lavender and thyme. Margaret envied the families: children laughing as the clouds broke up, boys pole-vaulting over a ditch in the distance.

A very large dog—as large as a small horse—was running as hard as it could, and the ram gave chase.

"He never tries to knock me down anymore," said Sister Barbara, as though an honor had passed her by. Margaret noticed that the nun did not refer to the ram by name—names were often considered sacred, and to give a Christian name like Fred to a beast was thought not entirely proper.

Some priories were busy places, filled with happy intrigue and industry, local merchants always arriving with carts of food and drink. Travelers often spent the night or at least a long meal enjoying good cheese and simple ale. This was a quiet refuge, made even more agreeable by the brazier of warm coals set beside them as they ate and the lilting, prayerful tune Sister Barbara hummed as she poured herself a cup of ale. Coals were rare in Margaret's experience—only the best houses had them. Silver cups gleamed on a shelf, and fine yellow candles stood in a row on a side table.

"We have a generous benefactor," said Sister Barbara, as though sifting Margaret's thoughts. "Our priory is dedicated to travelers in need, and we heal the soul of everyone who stays here."

"Margaret needs healing herself, having mated with that ram," said Bridgit. Nuns and priests brought out a coarse side of the lady's maid—Margaret had never understood why.

"This is not, I pray, a home for lazars," added Bridgit, with badly disguised distress. Lazars were decrepit folk, afflicted with skin diseases. Although the actual incidence of such skin ailments was rare, no one wanted to have contact with any knife or trencher that had been used by such pitiable souls.

Sister Barbara smiled. "Many summers ago, it used to be. The gifts of our generous patron have allowed us to cure a different sort of ill, with this ale from a brewer across the green and fresh fish from the streams."

"You are blessed to have such a protector," said Margaret.

The sister smiled and patted Margaret's hand. "And so are you. This is a refuge for people who have reason to be away from the daylight," she said with a meaningful glance. "The villagers will assume that you need God's peace."

Margaret did not know how to ask. "Is this a village of fierce farm animals?"

"And tremendous men, and terrifying women," said Sister Barbara. "Why do you ask?"

Margaret told the tale of the pig, as politely as possible, and added, "Folk across the land think Blackwell an ill, dangerous place; forgive me."

"We are pleased to keep our happiness a secret," said Sister Barbara. "All our pigs are fit and fat—and tame. Men saddle and ride them for sport."

Margaret closed her eyes and offered a heartfelt prayer for her father's safety, and for Robin Hood. And for Little John.

"We all come to holy poverty in the end," said Bridgit with a sigh as she examined the room they were to stay in for what John had called "a good handful of nights." A whitebeam-wood shelf supported a candle of pure white wax, and beige wool coverlets were folded on their sleeping pallets. The window shutter was open to the sunset. "They put us in a box and fold our hands, and we all lie as quiet as nuns."

"This is not poverty," said Margaret.

"No, but it is not a city dwelling, with a watchman and strong-armed neighbors."

"The ale was clear and pleasing," said Margaret, with more than a little irritation in her voice.

"You must forgive me, my lady, by my faith," said Bridgit at last, in an unfamiliar, almost humble tone.

Margaret had to ask with her eyes: Forgive you for what?

"For wanting everything done now, skinned and spitted," said Bridgit, reading her expression. It was an old formula, meaning over and done. "I wish us both safe in your father's house again, but I am learning patience from you."

Bridgit would have said more, but hooves sounded.

Margaret pressed against the door. Leather armor creaked, and the horses made the heavy, deep-lunged exhalations of steeds that had been ridden hard. A familiar male voice asked if any travelers had entered the priory that day.

"Today?" asked Sister Barbara in a suddenly quavering voice, as though she were frail beyond the power of speech. The priory was a traditional site of sanctuary, and Margaret and Bridgit would safe there—if the sheriff's men remained respectful of the law.

"This day, in the king's name," said the voice. Margaret recognized Nunna, trying to sound formal and sure of his own judgment.

"Today I took in a prayerful sick woman with lazar's

lesions," she said, "running with liquor like pink milk from every joint of her body."

"May the saints be merciful," said Nunna, sounding genuinely respectful toward the suffering poor, but discouraged, too, as though he had looked forward to searching the priory, sword in hand.

"I told you," said Wynbald, "that royal forester was mistaken. No forester has eyes in his head."

The bridle fittings chimed, hooves striking small pieces of gravel, the horses turning, sneezing, complaining as the men worked their mounts away from the disease-ridden priory.

When he had put some distance between himself and the priory, Nunna called out, "There wasn't a certain tall man in Lincoln green?"

"Man?" queried Sister Barbara.

But then the horses snorted and whinnied, Nunna swore, and Margaret could only guess what was happening: Old Fred protecting Blackwell from outsiders.

Margaret lay in the darkness. She was dressed in a linen gown, the cloth soft from summers of being laundered in the local streams.

Again she saw her husband's eyes, shining like agate stones, and as lifeless. She saw the broad oak stairway, and could picture clearly the tangle of drunken bodies, Henry the sheriff's man stirring, waking up as they passed.

"Do you remember—" Margaret began, reluctantly sharing a question with Bridgit. Margaret was unwilling to score the memory futher into her mind. "Do you remember one of the snoring bodies with a bloody sleeve?"

"I don't want to put such pictures into my sleep, my lady," said Bridgit from her pallet across the darkened room.

"Lying there drunk on the floor—"

"I remember the lot of them," sighed Bridgit. "An entire room of wine-slaughtered men, too horrible to look at."

"Think, Bridgit. Was it Hal or Lionel with blood up to his elbow?"

"Oh, it was bearded Lionel, my lady, his mouth looking like a gash in a blanket."

"Did Lionel take my husband's life?"

"All but certainly, my lady, but what does it matter? We can prove nothing, and Henry does not care a turnip's worth who really killed our poor, dear Sir Gilbert."

Margaret sat up in the darkness, her hand to her throat. "If we believe Lionel is guilty, then so must Henry."

"Of course, my poor dear lady," said Bridgit.

"You should have mentioned this, Bridgit, long before now."

"Henry doesn't care for the truth of the matter, my lady. He'll roast you over a fire just to get your father's silver, and your poor dead husband's, too."

Chapter 38

$\mathcal{J}$ohn captured a hare in his hand one dawn.

He did not reach out for it at once, but stayed still, watching the creature. John was hungry, and a roast hare would have been sweet that morning. He sat at the edge of a meadow, a clearing of thick grass going blond as the summer wore on. Nine coneys and two great hares partook of the green, nibbling and looking up with their dark eyes. Now and then a sound froze them.

There had never been such danger for Robin Hood and his men. The forest was thronged with man hunters, driven on by Henry. Rumored promises of rewards, and threats of punishment, had brought an especially skilled sort of tracker into the woods, armed with axes and hunting hounds. Henry was eager for more than the capture of the outlaws—he wanted Margaret Lea.

Now John crouched, alone except for the browsing rabbits and hares. The outlaws were scattered throughout the forest, and the silence told him that all was well. John breathed quietly, listening for the footsteps of deputies and the crash of their axes, cutting their way through deadfall and living thickets. But for the first morning in days, the woods were still.

A buck hare hobbled in that awkward-seeming way of the long-eared creatures. And the big man stretched out his hand and closed it around its ears.

The animal kicked and struggled, a blur, hind legs clawing at the air. John held the fighting buck hare well away from his body and waited until the creature ceased struggling, some instinct in the old hare making it still itself. Perhaps, John thought, such animals have a prayer they say, in their blood and in their bone, to the Lord in Heaven just before they die.

"Friend hare," said John solemnly. "Tell any power of these woods, whether divine or elven, that Robin Hood and his men are in hiding, and pray that the powers of the greenwood stand at their side."

Released, the hare scampered, zigzagged, and then leaped high over a log, his ears white in the sunlight.

John gathered Edwy and Carl Taw together and gave them a message to carry into the city.

Tell Henry Ploughman that I have something that belongs to the deputy.

Tell him I promise safe passage into the woods.

Chapter 39

That evening John stole through the trees, snaking under low branches, making his way across the bog where there was no track. When he stood at the edge of the village of Blackwell, he breathed the perfume of cooking fires and roast duck. Even the lowing of a cow made him feel an unaccountable peacefulness.

Old Fred was nowhere to be seen.

As soon as he entered the priory, John felt an unusual excitement.

Sister Barbara told him that the sheriff's men had visited Blackwell once again. "And this time they lanced the manure heaps, looking for you."

"Not a bad place to hide," said John with a smile, his eyes searching the candlelit corners as he wondered, Where is she?

"And a deputy used a long, sharp pole to probe the cesspit," said Sister Barbara. "They found the skeleton of a little dog."

"But no sign of Robin Hood," said John.

"Not that they could discover. But the sheriff's men did something they should not have done."

John guessed it before she spoke again.

Sister Barbara nodded. "Old Fred knocked a deputy down, and the man got to his feet and ran the breed-ram through with his sword."

Little John sighed. "The kingdom has lost a brave warrior."

"You look hungry, John."

"Not a bit," said John, a perfect lie. He wanted to blurt out, *Where is she? Where is Margaret?* But a surprising shyness kept the words from his lips.

"There's a great wheel of yellow cheese," Sister Barbara said. "Enough to kill a man, if it rolled on him."

"If we ate some," John suggested, "it would be that much less dangerous." He added, "And if we had help eating it, the work would go so much faster."

Margaret heard John's voice, and stopped before a blemished span of metal in an olive-wood frame. She peered at the image of a young woman that looked out at her.

"A lady should never make haste," cautioned Bridgit, "to meet a noble suitor."

"Little John is neither suitor nor nobleman," said Margaret.

But she did turn back to the hopeful vision in the priory's only mirror. What would the legendary outlaw see in her pale face and berry-blue eyes?

"If I did not know my lady better, by my faith," said Bridgit, "I would think John a loving earl, at the very least."

Margaret wanted to hear how Osric was faring, and Lucy, and all the others. John told her, and when he was done,

Margaret wished he would start all over and tell her again. But John explained that he had to make speed.

"I need to borrow something," he said. "Something that everyone in Nottingham would recognize as yours."

Margaret considered and then, with a whisper of cloth and a moment's struggle with the pin, placed her mother's brooch in his hand, the rubies and sapphires glittering.

John parted his lips. This was too valuable.

But he took it nonethless.

The moon was rising as John entered the forest, leaving the village with its homely smell of brewing yeast and cattle behind. What did it mean, he wondered, to feel so refreshed, so suddenly strong again? No doubt Sister Barbara's five-day ale was stronger than he thought. He carried a leather satchel of provisions, the finest white bread and wedges of cheese. "Saint Michael defend you," Margaret had said. *And come back soon.*

Moonlight seeped into the deep woods, making the shadows darker, illuminating the crook of a twig, the mossy knob of a stone. John traveled by memory, crouching and listening sometimes to sense the way. Owls coursed above the deer trails, and bats hunted, their wings leaving a wake of surprise and silence whenever they passed overhead. Was it John's confused imagination, still addled by rich cheese and strong ale, or did each flitting bat spell out a warning?

Chapter 40

$\mathcal{T}$he high, proud note of a horn rang out, and another nearby.

John had made a small camp in the shelter of a venerable oak that had long ago fallen and decayed into a protective hollow. A few sticks of dry wood and brown bracken fern flared up into a nearly smokeless fire.

Robin Hood bounded across a brook and hurried toward his tall friend.

"Henry Ploughman rides into the forest," said Robin, "with four spearmen."

Robin crouched in the hollow of the long-fallen oak, drinking from a skin of wine and water. Even though the outlaw leader had been tirelessly optimistic, his laugh always bright, a touch of weariness had begun to shade Robin's eyes in recent days. It made John feel all the more protective toward his friend.

"He comes in response to your message," said Robin, both statement and question. John had not discussed his plan, but little escaped Robin's attention.

John turned to a cache of weapons nestled in the hollow oak. He strapped on a broadsword, a fine weapon with the names of the Apostles minutely inscribed on the hilt and pommel. The sword had been bestowed upon the outlaws by a knight from Lastingham. Grimes kept an edge on it with a file and whetstone, but the blade was rarely used by any of the band.

John practiced drawing the weapon. The sword felt satisfying in his grip, he had to admit, and it would feel much better with the blade biting into the neck of Henry or Red Roger. A pattern-welded blade, half steel, half heavy iron— John wished he could flourish the weapon like a knight. But the only blade he had ever handled skillfully was a dressing knife, a two-handled tool for scraping hides, in his father's tannery.

"John, be careful," said Robin, climbing to his feet. The outlaw leader liked swordplay only in fun, as a sporting contest. "Whatever game you plan, Henry means harm."

The blade whispered, slipping back into its sheath. John unbuckled the weapon, and returned it to the shelter of the ancient tree. For a moment Robin was relieved, but then he saw the look in John's eye.

"Wear a horn at your hip, John," said Robin Hood. His eyes added, *If you will not change your mind.*

John took Grimes Black aside. He murmured instructions: what family of thatchers was kind along the High Way, which alewife was generous with her drink, where to find a good horse. And above all what message Grimes was to carry.

Henry was sweating in the sunlight, leaning forward in his saddle, wine sack swinging heavily at his side.

Four spearmen accompanied him, men with the thick necks and beefy shoulders of veteran castle guards. John stepped before the horsemen, directly in their path, but none of them saw John until the last moment.

They sawed at their reins, the horses snorting.

John leaned on his quarterstaff. "I have an understanding for you, Henry," John said. "For your ears alone."

Henry reached toward his belt, and John thought he was going to draw his sword. But he found his wine sack, lifted it, and drank without spilling a drop. His cheeks were fat with a mouthful, and he took a moment swilling the drink, considering. Then Henry urged the charger forward a few paces, and stopped.

John took the bridle in his hand.

"I know where the murderess is," said John in a low voice, when he had led the horse to the shadowy margin of the clearing.

"The dead knight's wench?"

"His widow," corrected John. He imagined how easy it would be to pluck this deputy from the saddle and slam him into the ground. But he kept his voice steady, maintaining his confiding tone. "I can take you to her."

Henry did not smile, and for a moment John could see the other, more simple man—a peasant's son, eager, proud to be a lawman, and frightened now that it all might slip away.

"Think of the silver you can extort from her," John added. "If she's in your grasp."

"Indeed," said Henry, his eyes alight with hope and caution. "Where is she?"

"Robin Hood knows nothing of this. He wants her treasure for himself. You understand how outlaws are."

Henry grunted.

"But I am like you, Henry," said Little John. "A simple man, but with my pride—weary of the devious ways of my master."

"Maybe you are a right worthy outlaw, after all," said Henry.

"I'll take you to her."

Henry considered this. "Good Little John, how do I know you have the spicer's daughter?"

John withdrew the jeweled brooch from his tunic. A ruby winked. "She did not part with this easily."

Henry ran his tongue over his lips. John could see it in his eyes—Henry saw a future again, winters of fat beef and sweet wine.

"How far away is she?" asked Henry.

"Far. And we must travel alone."

Henry could not take his eyes off the jewels.

John said, "Leave these men behind."

Henry laughed. "Pray tell me, why should I trust you?"

"If you agree, I'll give you this rich brooch." John loathed the thought of the jewels falling into Henry's broad hand. "A token of the riches to come."

"You do not love your master, Robin Hood," said Henry, in a tone of awakening insight. "You chafe under him—"

"Like you," said John, "I weary of a deputy's choice of table scraps and quartered pennies."

Henry laughed bitterly—but with growing warmth. "It's hard to be second in command, Little John. You and I have tasted that vinegar too long."

Little John knew then exactly how to win the trust of the lawman. "Robin Hood does not value my skill or my good name," said the big outlaw. "But I have a plan that will win you Margaret Lea's silver and at the same time play a worthy jest on my master."

Henry gave a low, thoughtful laugh. "A jest on Robin Hood! That would be a joy indeed."

"Years from now," said John, "there will be tales of how Henry the Cunning bested Robin Hood."

Henry savored the thought.

"The songs will call you Henry le Sly," John continued, "smarter than the wiliest thief who ever lived."

Henry leaned down from the saddle, lowering his voice. "What have you in mind?"

John spun a plan of deception and safe travel, with Margaret in Henry's hands at the journey's end.

"By Jesu, we are two men who think alike," said Henry.

"Very much alike," said John, perfecting his recitation of lies.

"But before I trust you," added Henry, "just as proof of your honor, I'll take that pretty brooch into my hand."

John climbed onto one of the spearmen's mounts, a stoical, stout riding horse, neither the finest sort of cob, nor the worst. The horse gave a wheezing sneeze at John's weight, but made no further complaint.

John hated the sight, Henry's hand closing around Margaret's brooch.

- Part Four -

FORBIDDEN FOREST

Chapter 41

The two of them covered miles.

John knew nothing of horses, but the cob was accustomed to bulky riders, it would seem, and followed the lead of Henry's charger.

By late afternoon it had begun to rain. Henry was outfitted in dark leather armor, with a close-fitting helmet over his head, a bowl of leather and iron. John offered his great green cloak to Henry, and he accepted it gratefully. As the rain grew heavy, and the two horsemen leaned into the wind, Henry said, "This is the sort of storm I came to Nottingham to escape."

"It doesn't rain within the city walls?"

Henry was hunched forward in his saddle, water dripping off the tip of his hood. "Not the way it rains down on a farmer and his brood, in a house made of mud and weeds. In winter there was frost on the cottage floor. And when the chickens pecked in and out of the doorway they scattered floor straw, and the straw caught fire from the hearth. My baby brother Arthur had a burn that turned blue and filled with pus. It killed him."

It was a common problem, infants and children burning to death in house fires, usually from open coals in the middle of a room. No doubt Henry had not intended to tell such a personal story—this bitter memory silenced him for a while.

Eventually Henry stirred himself to ask, "Do you keep holy days in the greenwood?"

The feast days, he meant—Candlemas, Easter, Michaelmas, and the like.

"For outlaws," said Little John, "every day is a feast."

When they reached an inn situated beside a parish church, Henry said that priest-brewed ale was good enough on such a night. Some churches and abbeys ran taverns as a way of funding church repairs and furnishing almshouses, but pilgrims and merchants sometimes complained that the drink served by a vicar's servant was little better than malt soup.

The Mitre and Hart was a cordial alehouse. A large fire blazed in the middle of the room, the flames spitting and sizzling as rain fought with them. Ale was served in mazers, ample wooden drinking bowls. Sweet grass was strewn liberally around the floor, and it was fresh, fine yellow hay, smelling of the open fields.

"Two horsemen such as yourself will have no trouble," said the innkeeper, a short, wiry man with a halo of yellow hair around a bald head.

"We'll have trouble if we want it," said Henry. "We're outlaws." Henry chuckled menacingly as he said this, but the innkeeper was neither startled nor amused. Traveling under this assumed identity, John believed, was the aspect of the journey that had most appealed to Henry.

"Oh, begging your pardon, sirs, I meant to remark to you

how well made you were, two such stout men as yourselves. Noble outlaws indeed, I said to myself as you stepped right in here, didn't I? I was going to warn you that all the roads north are held by robbers, Red Roger and his men."

"But I thought Red Roger's manor was well to the north," said John.

"Well to the north or not, as it may be," said the innkeeper. "But we hear Red Roger and his men are behind every tree, if it please you."

Henry gave the man a gentle, almost affectionate cuff. "Give us another bowl of ale, and don't scoop it from the bottom where all the wort settles."

"Outlaws are common as millers along the High Way, it seems," said Little John as the innkeeper scurried off.

"And about as honest," replied Henry.

The man returned with slabs of bread covered with hot, golden, bubbling cheese, fresh from the hearth. "No need to see a coin from either one of you, two fine men such as yourselves. Think of this as a gift from the parish of Saint Felix, and remember us if you feel the need."

The need for what? John wondered.

"Look here, my man," said Henry, sounding much like a man of the city. "We're not outlaws at all. See this fine black leather under my cloak, and this fine deputy of mine, big as three haywards."

The innkeeper straightened, and showed his teeth in a cautious smile.

"We're sheriff's men!" said Henry, slapping the table.

The innkeeper retired into the flickering shadows, and returned with another pitcher of foaming ale.

"We're lawmen!" chortled Henry, looking around at the drinking men and women along the wall. "And we drink wine."

"If you want any coin from us you'll have to wait until harvest," said the innkeeper. "We're poor folk until then."

"Do a sheriff's man and an outlaw take from the same purse?" asked Henry, with something like real surprise.

"Indeed, if you'll forgive me," said the innkeeper. "We of Saint Felix stay well away from both. But if you are lawmen, then I'm a griffin."

Henry and Little John had to share a bed, a flat pallet stuffed many summers ago with summer grass, but now worn as hard as earth. It was usual for travelers to share a bed, although not always comfortable, and John lay listening to the deep, ragged snores of his companion. The rain hammered at the shutters outside, and a trickle of water began to drum in a corner of the room. Henry had drunk currant wine, gooseberry wine, blackberry and rowan wine, and then, announcing that grape wine was all that suited him, drank a seeming hogshead of that.

When he spoke in his sleep he was arguing, whining, telling a dream combatant, "Put it down, please. No, please put it down—don't hurt me."

John rose from the pallet and stepped softly to the shuttered window. *Go back, go back,* said the water streaming from the eaves.

Henry sobbed in his sleep.

The guttering rain warned John, but it did not say where he should go. Back to Sherwood Forest? Back to Lord Roger? Or all the way back—to York, to the streets of his childhood, where he had cured hides with his father, scattering dog dirt on the toughest ox hides to help soften them into leather.

John opened the shutters and breathed the fragrance of wet leaves. He knew that what he had in mind was wrong, even sinful. But he considered Margaret in Henry's grasp, and

Osric in pain yet again from another beating—or dead. John knew the countryside suffered under Henry, with no one strong enough to break him.

Forgive me, Heaven, prayed John, for what I am about to do.

Forgive me; and whatever happens to me—keep Margaret safe.

Chapter 42

*R*ain fell over the priory roof in the darkness. It made a soothing whisper, but Margaret was not asleep.

She knew that somewhere in the darkness Little John was hiding from Henry and his fellow deputies, and Margaret prayed that Saint Christopher—himself a giant—might protect the young man. And let her see him again.

The sound of horses had awakened her. Two horses were somewhere outside, their hooves scuffing the gravel beyond the priory walls. Only two mounts, not enough to be a gang of deputies this time of night. And yet her pulse quickened.

What would she use as a weapon, if she needed one? Her hand found a silver pitcher and an earthenware jug. She imagined swinging the jug, breaking it over a deputy's head. But then she put it down, unable to breathe.

She heard something. A voice.

A voice from the rain outside touched her, a male query: "Are we here?"

She was out of bed, hurrying into a mantle.

A fist knocked on the door, and she hesitated. Surely, she thought, this was how Henry would arrive to capture her at last.

Bridgit was awake, using a bellows on the embers in the brazier, the coals brightening. "Only a heathen would be out in such weather," said Bridgit. "Or a devil." She called after Margaret to wait, but it was too late.

Something very like a familiar voice had reached Margaret yet again. She wasn't certain. She did not want to give in to hope—fear of disappointment made her caution herself. But she could not keep her feet from racing into the dark outer rooms.

Sister Barbara, fully dressed and carrying a smoking tallow lamp, was already at the heavy door, asking who needed Christian refuge on this wet night.

"A knight of his word," said a familiar foreign accent, "bringing a traveler from London."

Sir Marco stood aside with a smile, and William Lea stepped into the shifting circle of lamplight, his eyes searching, afraid to have faith in this unfamiliar place, and afraid to believe that what was happening could be trusted.

And then he saw Margaret and she was in her father's arms, his muddy cloak enclosing her, his arms wrapping her, a thankful prayer on his breath.

Chapter 43

When the two men left the inn the next dawn, John paused before climbing onto the heavy-boned horse. The previous day's journey had made him stiff and sore in hip and thigh, and Little John relished a moment longer on his two feet.

The innkeeper held the cob steady, unnecessarily—the horse was well-mannered and resigned. But the man was eager to give the best possible last impression, offering them a gift of dried fish, knotted into lengths like rope. "So you will think well of us on your way back," said the innkeeper.

"If anyone asks," said John in a low voice, leaning down from the saddle, "tell them Robin Hood and Little John were your guests last night."

The innkeeper's eyes grew round. But then with a sly cock of his head he said, "But I think I did guess, by my faith."

"Did you?"

"Robin Hood I would not have known," he said. "But no one in the kingdom could mistake you, Little John."

"How much farther?" asked Henry in a cadaverous voice. John shook his head—he didn't know.

"My skull is packed with gravel," Henry moaned.

The previous night's rain had passed, leaving the sky empty blue. Over the hours of hard road, riding into the north wind, John felt his body grow cold to the marrow with the chilly weather and with doubt. Such wind made no reassuring murmur, and the only birds he saw were sparrows, struggling to keep a perch on bobbing ditch weeds, their feathers awry with the breeze. Henry huddled in his woodsman's cloak, looking like any traveler—or any outlaw.

Henry was already weighing the leather sack of wine, sloshing it, looking at John with an unspoken offer. The innkeeper had filled it that morning from a pipe of wine "shipped all the way from Honfleur, not a fortnight past." Henry drank and coughed.

"This good wine is fit for Holy Mass," Henry said.

John took a taste, and the red wine was as good as the drink Robin Hood had taken from a royal chamberlain last Saint Stephen's Day.

Little John tried to assuage his private fears that the trap might fail. What was John to do if Grimes had not reached Lord Roger's manor? Or if Lord Roger was out riding the hills, not to be reached? Or—and this was very likely—Lord Roger got Grimes's message, and did not believe it? John could imagine his laugh, and see his skeptical smile as he cautioned the outlaw to run back to Sherwood Forest before a hound lapped him off the floor. If Red Roger and his men did not mistake Henry for Robin Hood, the trap would fail.

The sunlight was weak, each breath of cold wind harsh. The road was too empty. Congregations of blackbirds gathered along the water-filled road ruts and scattered only as the two approached. It had been a long time since John had realized how lone and bereft a traveler could feel. There were no other folk on the High Way, neither tinker nor carter.

Dark gray sheep grazed on either side of the road by late morning, the field as close-cropped as any penitent's scalp. A peasant near the road labored with a hack, a crude hoe with a large, irregular iron blade. The wind was growing calm, and the sky was more than blue—a deep, perfect void.

John wished the peasant a good morning. But as he spoke he ran his eye over the hills, the line of royal forest, the green carpet of sheep-cropped field. It was the absence of life that caught his attention.

"See what's there," Robin Hood had taught Little John. "And what isn't."

The hedges were too silent. The starling and blackbird were still. The rooks in the spreading oaks were high up in the branches, as though something had passed beneath them, sending them scrambling higher for safety.

The peasant wore patched leather shoes and a tattered tunic, shiny with soil. He did not speak. He lifted his eyebrows, and sent a message with his glance at Little John: *danger.*

Henry rode over to the man and aimed a kick at the peasant's head, his foot barely missing. "Who do you think you're looking at, you turd hoggler?" demanded Henry, knocking the peasant to the ground.

Men of such a lowly order in life rarely looked travelers directly in the eye—it was considered impolite. Henry tried to straddle the peasant with his horse, attempting to force the animal to tread on the cowering field man. "You have no business," said Henry, "lifting your ignorant eyes at us."

"No, my lord," said the peasant's muffled voice, "indeed I do not."

The horse was nearly as upset as the field man, the steed rolling its eyes, unwilling to step on the quivering human figure. John seized the bridle and pulled Henry and his mount back into the road.

"Our apologies, good man," said Little John. "My companion has all the sense of a goose."

"Why do you waste apologies on this land man?" demanded Henry heatedly. "He needs a lesson in keeping to his station."

There was a sound, the sort of tiny *tick* a blade makes grazing stone.

The peasant had dropped his hack. Now he leaped to his feet and ran. He was careful to keep away from the puddles as he leaped low rills and culverts across the green.

Henry observed this and gazed around at the sunny forenoon. The anger vanished from his eyes, and was replaced with a keen suspicion.

"You believe yourself superior to me," said Henry, "possessing a wiser heart and a keener eye—don't you, John?"

Little John made no response, aware of the spreading silence of the grazing land around them.

"I myself know who stabbed Sir Gilbert with a pretty knife," said the deputy. "I saw who did it with these very eyes in my head."

John could not keep the eager curiosity from his voice. "Every outlaw in the woods knows you're a worthy opponent." The truth regarding the murder, John knew, could place Margaret beyond all harm.

"Do they indeed?" asked Henry, boyish in his willingness to believe. Then he sighed.

"It was Lionel the shield bearer who took his master's life because the worthy knight tossed a pair of weighted dice."

John smiled. Once word of Margaret's innocence was spread, no deputy could lay hand on her.

A small sound—a tick, a pebble grating under a heel—made John straighten in his saddle. Henry heard it, too, but without any show of anxiety. He groped for his sword.

A head bobbed from behind a stone wall. A shoulder showed for an instant over a hedge. Shrubs trembled. Spearheads glinted. John's stout-legged cob shied at movement from behind.

The first spear cracked into the small of Henry's back.

It knocked him off his mount. The sheriff's man tried to reach around and seize the weapon, but another spear struck his head, knocking the helmet awry and sending blood down his features. Henry staggered to his feet, and then each new spear drove air from his body, gushes of wordless sounds, until the sheriff's man collapsed on the road, face down in the mud. His attackers finished him, wrenching their spears and plunging them in again, wetting their spearheads with crimson.

Heaven forgive me, prayed John, aghast at the sight of bright lung blood spraying from Henry's lips. Then, as a spearhead stabbed into Henry's neck and another gouged the deputy's face, John could not stand it any longer.

He rode his mount into the knot of armed men, striking about him with his staff. One spearhead ripped his mantle, and a spear shaft grazed his head, half stunning him for an instant.

"Robin Hood is dead!" cried a spearman, rising up from Henry's crumpled form.

Chapter 44

The spearmen formed a circle around Little John. Each spear was held in gloved hands, each man leather-armored, the brass studs and fittings polished. Several of the spears were winged—fitted with a metal flange so the head could penetrate only so far into man or beast.

Nine spearmen, thought Little John. Only nine, and a mangy bunch they were too, swollen with drink, panting with effort. In other circumstances John would have pitied them. These were not sharp-eyed poachers like Tom Dee. Tavern louts, bullies, strong-arm robbers—these were the best Red Roger could get.

The nobleman rode from across a field, his red silk sleeves brilliant in the light. He made a wide circuit, leaped a wall, and let his horse slow to an easy pace. The bridle fittings were polished brass, and a yellow hemp rope hung coiled from the saddle. Red Roger parted the spearmen, and took a long moment to let his horse exhale and inhale, a man kind to his mount.

He spoke softly—John had almost forgotten how quietly

he could speak. "I knew you'd come back to me, John, even after all this time." His lean features were more gaunt, but he still gave that thin smile, like a priest with a regretfully sinful flock.

"I gave your man Grimes a gold mark," Red Roger continued. "More money than he will see in ten years. And I let him go."

Red Roger stayed on horseback, using the butt of a spear to lever Henry's body slowly, laboriously, onto his side, and then all the way over. The deputy's face was white and inert in the noon sun, and John offered a silent prayer for his soul.

"Mine was the thrust that killed him," said a corpulent spearman. "I win the purse of coin."

Red Roger gazed at Henry, peering down, prodding with the shaft of his spear. Then he looked up, his eyes meeting John's gaze. When he spoke, it reminded John of a holy man about to deliver a Lenten homily, frowning to let sinners know that sobering words were about to follow.

"Who is this man?" asked Red Roger quietly.

"I killed Robin Hood!" insisted the burly spearman.

John kicked the cob hard, and the broad-chested horse lurched into a spearman, knocking him down and planting a hoof on the man's chest. Then the horse stumbled, knocked over another spearman, and slipped, a hoof seeking solid footing and finding only scrambling arms and legs. It fell, rolling, dumping John.

The big man was on his feet at once. He knocked a winged spear to one side, kicked a lunging spearman in the face. Whipping the quarterstaff in a quick half circle, he knocked a thin, nimble spearman to the ground. He stabbed the end of the staff hard into the chest and belly of another armed man.

But several more attackers surrounded John, goading him with their spears. John struck one of them so hard the man's knees buckled, but an iron point ripped into his thick wool tunic. John blocked the man in the face with a cross blow, and heard Red Roger laugh.

John sent a prayer to the hills and the fields, the hedges and the stones, and to whatever ancient spirits dwelled there. He did not dream that this green country had any power that could save his life.

And yet he asked.

John stumbled, glanced down, and found the peasant's hack in his hands, damp with field mud, a great single tooth of iron. He drove the blade into the shoulder of a stout spearman. As a thrown spear missed John by a handsbreadth, the big outlaw struck out, snapping spear shafts, parrying swords, until at last the shaft of the hack broke, sending the head spinning.

Men fled. John retrieved his staff from the hoof-scarred road and climbed into the saddle of his startled, foaming mount.

Lord Roger drew his sword. It was a well-kept weapon, bright blue in the daylight. Then, like any nobleman deciding the day's hunt was too dull, he slid the sword back into its brunette leather sheath. He wheeled and rode off, leaping a hedge of wild rose and hazelwood.

John followed, his horse barely clearing the hedge. It landed heavily, and then rocked into a gallop as Red Roger vanished into the copse at the top of the hill.

Chapter 45

This was not the stately woodland of Sherwood Forest, but it was all royal hunt land, low trees and gorse. John's horse labored under the big man's weight, but he urged the sweating animal forward, over hummock and shrub.

Branches lashed the outlaw as he rode, and his horse slowed down as the thick nettles and dry, spongy peat land alternated, pine and berry bushes blocking the twisting trail. John reined in his mount and listened. He heard the thudding hooves of Red Roger's horse, and then silence.

Breath heaved in and out of the cob as John let the beast rest for a few heartbeats, and then the animal gave a groan as John urged it forward.

John saw the rope stretched across the trail at the last moment. It was too late to duck his head. The taut line of rope caught him in the throat, and he felt his body lift up out of the saddle. John crashed heavily to the woodland floor.

Red Roger was a heartbeat too slow in hurrying from the shadows. John had time to climb to one knee, gasping, clutching at his throat. He had enough time to find his quarterstaff and reckon his chances, staff against sword.

Red Roger hesitated.

The hesitation allowed Little John time to drive the end of the staff into Red Roger's ribs, knocking the lean swordsman back, and back again as the bigger man maneuvered. John knew from sword practice with Grimes Black that a staff could be hacked in half easily by a broadsword, and he also knew that the nobleman was not as strong as he was cunning.

It was no surprise when Red Roger gave a few lunges and retreated, back uphill through the low branches, John slogging forward through the wet ground, raising an arm to keep the branches from whipping his eyes. And when he took a step back, unwilling to continue this uphill trudge, Red Roger thrust, and thrust again, cutting a new rip in John's tunic, drawing blood from his arm.

So it is with cunning men, thought John as he dodged a broadsword flourish. They know how to make a game of everything they do. John lumbered forward again, ducking, plodding, the swordsman making John expend all the effort. Roger's lean, aquiline features were alight with a kind of joy.

John saw it long before they were close: the carefully layered grasses out of place in the ferns of the woodland floor. *A mantrap.* The big man was nearly out of breath, following the parrying nobleman up the faint deer trail, the heavy sword biting notches from John's staff until it was cut in two.

Out of breath as John was, he gave a resigned laugh. It was a harsh, rasping sound—his throat was raw where the rope had cut him. I am more clever than I used to be, thought Little John, but still not clever enough.

The laugh made Red Roger stop midfeint, a question in his eyes.

Little John stepped into Roger, seized his sword hand, and held it. He gripped hard, squeezing until the knuckles of Red Roger's hand compressed, bones and cartilage cracking. The nobleman gave a gasp, but would not let his weapon fall.

John knocked the nobleman to the leaf meal and kicked the sword across the ground, the spinning blade winking into the shadows.

A dagger, tugged quickly from his horse-leather leggings, flashed in Red Roger's hands, and only John's reflexes kept the blade from slicing his hands, his wrists.

Roger's eyes darted to the bone-handled knife at John's hip. "Knife to knife," said Roger. "I'll teach you yet, John."

John took one moment to slip the hunting blade from its sheath. It was no match for the longer weapon in Red Roger's hand. As John settled the blade in his hand, Red Roger took one step back, and another, light-footing his way up the gentle slope, onto the mantrap.

Before Little John could cry out a warning, the cover of the trap fell in with a crash, and Red Roger vanished.

Chapter 46

Red Roger struggled, but could not not pry his body free.

Ash stakes thrust up around his form, through him. In the darkness of the mantrap, treetops and portions of sky began to gleam, reflected in Red Roger's spreading blood.

Little John lowered himself slowly, carefully, down into the pit, and knelt among the sharpened stakes, blood quaking around him. He put a hand on Red Roger's quick points, the places in his neck and wrists where life pulses, and felt only ebbing strength.

The noble outlaw had much to atone for, and John offered a prayer that Roger's soul might find peace. John knew that someday he would recall the noble adversary with the respect such a tireless opponent deserves. But now John was swept with the strongest sensation of relief. The feeling was so strong that he remained where he was for a long moment, steadying himself against the damp wall of the pit.

Then John stretched to his full height, and clung to the edge of the mantrap. He pulled himself out into the day.

John's horse waited at the faint trace, the barest hint of a path. With a whispered apology for taxing the animal's endurance further, John mounted the cob and rode back down the slope.

Henry's body lay where John had left it, its fists clutched in the scarlet mud.

John knelt, hesitating at the sight of the wounds. Then he searched the deputy's clothing for the brooch. The deputy's tunic was laden with hidden pouches: Flemish gold in one leather sack, and a skinner's knife in a sheath stitched next to Henry's ribs. The man had been a walking tier of hidden pokes and purses, worn silver and newly minted coin hidden beneath his clothes. Further weapons fell out, too, as the big outlaw searched—a dirk and a poniard sticky with blood.

But no sign of the brooch.

A falcon lifted high over the hillcrest and fell away to the far side, leaving the sky empty. If any creature or woodland power watched from the spine of the hills, or from the lichen-splashed stones of the pasture, John could not detect it.

And he was not sure he wanted to. "Never look hard where you think they're hiding," Hilda used to advise.

"Where is it?" whispered John.

The wind sighed through the long, sheep-shorn field. Perhaps it was John's imagination, or some power in the field offered advice.

Jewels gleamed through Henry's fingers, and John retrieved the brooch from the dead man's grasp. John looked down at the vacant face of the deputy. He imagined the mortally stricken Henry searching his pockets as he died, retrieving the jewel from a hiding place in his clothing, bringing it out so he could relish the sight of it at the end.

The tall outlaw untied the knot that fastened the horn to

his belt. Even a knot could loose magic into the world around it, so Little John breathed a prayer. With his throat throbbing, and his mouth dry, it was no surprise when he could sound nothing more than a thin, rude bleat.

He licked his lips. Again he pressed the horn to his mouth, and this time the note was like a gander's hiss, a pathetic *blat*, even weaker than before.

John found Henry's goatskin of wine, slashed and empty, except for a few scant swallows that he let trickle between his lips. He filled his lungs with air—three, four deep breaths. And this time when he put the horn to his lips, he did not force the note.

And when it sounded it was a sour, strangled sound—except for the very last instant, when one pure note lifted up into the wind. John sounded it again, the same note, fuller this time, and louder. And again. The hillside echoed, the rooks fell silent, the tit-birds and the linnets rapt under the commanding, single note that Little John sent high into the blue.

John's mind played a trick—he seemed to hear a tantalizing note echoing his. Soon Red Roger's toughs would ride down the hill again, drawing steel from sheath. His mind betrayed him yet again—another haunting, sweet-sounding horn.

For what felt like an age, John stood beside the broken body of the lawman, eyeing the field for signs of Red Roger's men.

Then a cart squeaked and groaned over the crest in the road, oxen plodding briskly, wheels rolling serenely along the muddy High Way. A driver trotted beside the beasts, and a hooded, round-backed carter leaned forward on his perch, the sort of stolid, world-weary man who cares nothing for sun or rain. The load of stacked flour sacks was barely restrained by the ropes, the freight about to tumble. The cart took little time to roll up from the south—the oxen were shuffling along at a fresh pace they would not be able to maintain for long.

As the load approached, the carter called out a long, low syllable, and the cart creaked to a standstill.

The carter threw back his hood, straightened his back, and Robin Hood jumped down from the perch. Flour sacks broke open, and Alan Red, Grimes Black, and Lucy spilled onto the road, stretching and beaming at the sight of the open sky.

Robin Hood took John's arm. "You're unhurt, John," said the outlaw leader, half assertion, half question. Robin Hood's smile could not disguise his concern.

"Are you surprised to see me standing?" said John.

"Every day should surprise," said Robin Hood, with a laugh, as he embraced his friend.

Chapter 47

$\mathcal{G}$eoffrey, the lord sheriff of Nottingham, poured them each another cup of green wine.

"And for your troubles," said the sheriff, "no doubt Heaven will repay you."

Margaret had held the rapt attention of the sheriff and her father, telling a tale both truthful and incomplete, of gentle outlaws, safe but unnamed hiding places, and a relentless deputy. She had spent only one night here in the city, and her sleep had been broken by dreams of trees stirring, and the soft laughter of sentries in the woods.

The sheriff laughed sadly. "Henry would face the most flinty justice," he said, "if he had lived."

The castle around Margaret whispered with the steps of servants, and the high, oak-beamed ceilings were the stuff of ballads, the sort of strong-walled keep where ladies awaited lovers. But how still the air in such a room, she thought, and how muted the distant murmur of the birds.

"I myself have word from the greenwood," said the sheriff.

"You must tell us!" prompted Margaret's father.

"Lionel Ogbert, shield bearer to your worthy husband," began the sheriff, after hesitating. Fine manners and compassion made him pause again, and then he continued, "Lionel took Sir Gilbert's life in a gamblers' dispute."

"How did you discover the truth?" Margaret heard herself ask in a whisper.

"People come and go from the greenwood," said the sheriff. "With a word for my ear, from time to time."

"Which one of the outlaws brought you this news?" asked Margaret.

"It was a message from Little John," said the sheriff, "given to me by the quick-eyed, toothless man called, I believe, Will Scathlock."

Margaret was surprised at how she felt just then. If John himself had visited Nottingham, without an opportunity for her to see him—the thought was painful.

Chapter 48

The streets of Nottingham seemed crowded to Margaret. And how narrow the passageways, a dung heap beside every door. She made her way beside her father, but she felt how shrunken and gray she was becoming, moment by moment, no longer simply Margaret, among friends in the wood, but Widow Margaret.

"I suppose it's our duty to attend," said her father, making his way beside her in the street.

"People will expect to see us there," offered Margaret.

Two days had passed since their meeting with the sheriff. She had been waking at night, alive with the impression that she was in the forest, with Little John nearby, only to fall back into the bedding, hearing the watchman's singsong. Bridgit was pleased to be within walls and even now bustled among laundry and servants. "The forest was all very well," Bridgit had said, "but my dream has always been to serve my lady in a great house."

Margaret feared that she might live for decades now, a remnant, well provided for but clothed in shades of gray and black, as was proper for widows. She might even inherit her husband's dwelling, under her father's guidance, as the law provided. William had been sitting, goose quill in hand, making inventories of new spices he expected from London any day. Margaret knew that she would see flowers only in the marketplace, and great oaks only from afar. And when, she wondered, would she ever again hear laughter?

She would live like this, she counseled herself. She would learn to be happy. All manner of things were fair, and each of Margaret's prayers had been answered.

Except for the return of the brooch.

Soon, she trusted, one of the outlaws would bring it back to her. And there was one other private prayer that went unfulfilled—she wished she could look into Little John's eyes.

Ralf the pie man had a stall near the wall. Tom Finch, the baker, had made special cakes for the occasion, half-moon shapes flavored with honey and cloves. The cakes were delicious, and Margaret enjoyed two of them. But she felt that she did not need to learn a lesson from any sinner's punishment on this cool, sunny day. The streets were thronged with field men and their wives, with purses heavy with farthings. The air was rich with flavor like the inside of a mill, the faint perfume of wheat and barley in each breath.

The lord sheriff and his young assistant, Hugh, were on horseback, showing the law's authority in their expensive dark armor. The chief lawman gave a nod to her father, and William wished the sheriff good day. The lawman gazed down at Margaret and smiled. "It is good to see you well, Margaret."

"And you, Lord Sheriff," said Margaret. She was grateful to the sheriff for his gentleness, but she knew, too, that he represented all that the outlaws did not.

This is how she would live now, bound by high manners.

It would be well—she would not suffer. But the great oaks of the woodland beyond were turning autumn russet, the first few leaves drifting, then lofting upward with a breeze. A band of royal foresters guarded the verge of the timberland, and here in full daylight it was clear how richly dressed they were, their green tunics freshly brushed, their leggings soft-cured, knife pommels gleaming.

Margaret did not like to set eyes on her husband's killer. Despite all her prayers, she could not bring herself to forgive such a crime. Nor did she take pious satisfaction at the thought of his punishment. She pitied Sir Gilbert for having had such an untrustworthy shield bearer, and silently prayed for the repose of her husband's soul.

Henry Ploughman was dead—many citizens had seen the cart that brought his body to the city gates. The entire town was quietly joyful at his demise.

And now the crowd hushed. The wheelers were at their duty, the huge stone wheel rolling silently across the field. The wheel was rolled into place near the tethered man. The bearded Lionel was weeping, asking for Nottingham's mercy. The throng stirred, murmuring, displeased at this poor beginning to Lionel's penance. The dark-clad man went silently about his duties, tightening leather thongs, eyeing his work, hands on his hips. He held out a hand, asking the wheelers to wait—all was not right.

Her father shook his head. "Margaret, I cannot watch," he said in an apologetic whisper, and made his way toward the edge of the crowd.

The executioner plucked a few blades of grass out of the likely path of the wheel and stepped on the turf to make sure it was firm, intent on further minute adjustments of the wooden frame and the knots. Lionel was crying out, and the crowd did not approve, murmuring. The wheel had not yet begun its service, and Lionel Ogbert was bawling.

Margaret closed her eyes. It was punishing to hear this broad-shouldered criminal begging, "If you will do it—hurry."

The executioner did not like the way the wheel had been polished and took a long moment to wipe the rim with his own hands, using an oiled cloth, his assistants rolling the huge disk with effort. At last the iron rim gleamed under Nottingham's careful attention.

He folded the cloth. He gave a nod, and the priest began to read the Latin prayers, lifting his voice over Lionel's sobs. The crowd's silence took on a special weight. Women held up infants so that even the very young could take in God's justice.

The wheel descended the gentle slope, and approached the tethered sinner.

A touch at her sleeve.

She turned, and a familiar smile met her.

"Osric!"

The juggler put a finger to his lips. "There are more king's men than ever in the woods," said Osric. When the hood slipped back, she could see the neat scar along his scalp, healing well. "New men, with new-made crossbows."

It was not far between the field of worshipful folk and the greenwood. Just a few long strides. But she had to be quick, lest the band of royal foresters spy them. The forest cool closed in around her, the sudden dark so complete after the bright sun that at first she could not see.

Rubies and sapphires reflected the shadowy light descending from the trees.

Little John held the brooch in his outstretched hand.

Chapter 49

She had forgotten so soon how tall John was, and how his eyes took on the green glow of the canopy of early autumn trees. She ran her gaze over his new-cut staff, and the horn at his belt. Margaret wanted to stay where she was, never see another wheeling or another blackened skeleton on a gibbet as long as she lived.

"I'll not be happy," said Little John, "until you pin the jewel to your mantle."

"Then you will not be happy, John."

The tall outlaw blinked—he did not understand. Will Scathlock leaned on a longbow, a splash of sunlight falling across his hopeful features.

"You forget, John," Margaret continued, "that each visitor is asked to leave a bit of treasure in the greenwood."

John gave a gentle laugh but shook his head.

"Each guest," added Margaret, "leaves a toll."

"But you are not a guest," said Little John.

"Am I an outlaw, John?"

The big outlaw lifted his chin, eyes alive to the distant murmur of a forester. And again Margaret felt how town-bound she had become in just a few days as a thrill, something like joy, swept over her. And something like fear too. The woods were heavy with secrets.

A long cry reached her from Lazarfield, Lionel baying under the punishment that, now begun, could endure for hours.

Robin Hood stepped from the shadows and gave a low whistle. Will Scathlock shrank behind a berry bush and was gone, and for an instant Margaret did not realize what was happening. Robin Hood vanished, too, only to reappear nearby.

A royal forester knelt in the trail, the bright cockade in his cap catching the light. He crept forward, step by step, following Margaret's footprints. Three more men joined him, and one of the king's men shrugged the crossbow from his back.

"There they are."

A forester's whisper. The crossbow was lifted and aimed in the direction of the three outlaws. But a branch snagged the weapon. A long, golden-leafed oak clung to the bow as the king's man cursed.

The great oaks arched overhead as Margaret ran, Little John at her side, following Robin Hood into the forest.